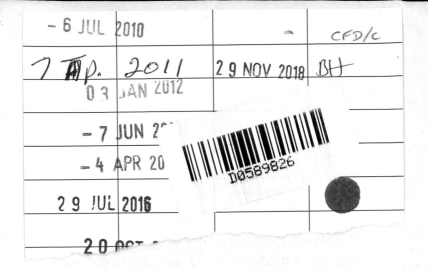

PHOENIX IN THE ASHES

Paul Varonne had been dead for six months, yet at Château Varonne reminders of him were still evident. Living there was his mother, who still believed him alive and Chantal, his amoral cousin. Into this brooding atmosphere comes Paul's widow, Francesca, after a nervous breakdown. When she meets Peter Devlin, an Englishman staying in the village, it seems that happiness is within her grasp — until she learns the staggering truth about the château and its inhabitants.

*Books by Georgina Ferrand
in the Linford Romance Library:*

THE GILDED CAGE
ASSIGNMENT IN VENICE
THE BECKONING DAWN
AZTEC WEDDING
MOON MARRIAGE
LAND OF EUCALYPTUS
TROUBLE IN PARADISE

GEORGINA FERRAND

◆

PHOENIX IN THE ASHES

Complete and Unabridged

LINFORD
Leicester

First published in Great Britain in 1974 by
Robert Hale Ltd
London

First Linford Edition
published 2008
by arrangement with
Robert Hale Ltd
London

British Library CIP Data

Ferrand, Georgina
  Phoenix in the ashes.—Large print ed.—
  Linford romance library
  1. Love stories
  2. Large type books
  I. Title
  823.9'14 [F]

  ISBN 978–1–84782–261–1

Published by
F. A. Thorpe (Publishing)
Anstey, Leicestershire

Set by Words & Graphics Ltd.
Anstey, Leicestershire
Printed and bound in Great Britain by
T. J. International Ltd., Padstow, Cornwall

1

'*Je voudrais louer une auto.*'

Francesca repeated the sentence from her phrase-book; she repeated it slowly and as she did so a feeling of frustration bordering on panic began to mount inside her. The familiar sensation of banging her head uselessly against a metaphoric wall came back to her, and as if she experienced a sudden pain she gasped.

All that the careful phrases, rehearsed silently during the journey, had elicited was a stream of rapid French she couldn't hope to understand.

'I want to hire a car — *une auto*,' she said again, mouthing each syllable as if she were addressing an idiot — a deaf idiot at that. 'Do you understand what I'm saying?'

The Frenchman was standing behind a desk strewn with colourful brochures.

1

All around them the din in the airport terminal was deafening, adding to Francesca's growing frustration.

The man's expression remained bland, indicating that he had been involved in this kind of situation before. Awkward tourists were no novelty to him.

'I understand perfectly, *mademoseille*,' he replied without surrendering an ounce of his calm. 'I am chosen for this job because I speak English. However, I regret that there simply is no automobile available. I cannot give you what I do not have. *Comprenez?*'

'But this is where cars are hired. If I can't get a car *here* where can I get one from?'

The clerk this time allowed his face to crack into the smallest smile. 'I will endeavour to explain, *mademoiselle*; we have only so many automobiles for hire and today they are all booked. Tomorrow morning, however, I will have cars.' He glanced up and down the chart before him on the desk. 'Let me see now. Ah, yes, you may choose from a

Citroen and a Renault tomorrow morning.'

He looked at her in the manner of a man bestowing a treat upon a child.

Francesca closed her eyes. Her hands curled into fists on top of the desk. 'Tomorrow is no good,' she said through clenched teeth.

'I am sorry, *mademoiselle*.' The look of long-suffering patience had returned to the clerk's pinched features. 'It would have been better if you had arranged to hire the car before you left London. That is how it is done if the matter is urgent. Why not spend the night in Bordeaux? It is a lovely city — second only to Paris in beauty, so some say. Tomorrow you can have a car. I will reserve it for you now.'

Giving her no chance to reply, the clerk moved along the desk to attend to someone else.

Francesca turned round and sank back against the desk as if her legs would no longer support her weight. They were trembling slightly and she had the insane desire to scatter all those mockingly colourful brochures with one sweep of her hand, and wipe the complacent smile from the clerk's face.

Useless to explain to this man that tomorrow just would not do. Tomorrow her courage might have evaporated completely.

She looked up and caught sight of her own face in a mirror. In the past six months it had fined down; shadows and hollows that hadn't been there before gave it new facets. She put one hand up to her cheek where the skin was stretched taut across her bones; it was warm and slightly moist.

Someone hurried past, almost knocking her off balance. He steadied her, apologised in French, and was gone.

A moment later she straightened up, calm again. She was stupid to become flustered by so small a matter. Of course she should have arranged for the hire of a car in London. Tonight she would stay in Bordeaux and tomorrow, refreshed again, she could drive to St. Marcel.

She stole a glance at herself in the mirror again. Yes, I look quite ordinary, she thought. Normal. Just a girl with ash blonde hair and dark grey eyes which were too big now for that fine-boned face. A girl who wore last year's coat although it was now too big for her slender frame. A girl who was twenty-three years old and looked not a day over seventeen.

It was that very childlike quality about her that Paul had always loved, and, in her turn, she had responded to his worldliness and sophistication and the protection he offered.

They had been together for five short years and to Francesca there had been no other life; there could be no other life.

The emptiness still persisted. The doctor said it would pass. She supposed it would. The other feelings had. She glanced around her. There were hundreds of people rushing to and fro; not one of them took any notice of her. No one gave her so much as a glance.

Despite the warmth of the terminal building she shivered. Incredible to believe she had been that woman on the brink of insanity. When she looked back on those nightmare months it was as if a film were unfolding in front of her, showing her events that had happened to someone else. Now it was difficult to recall that feeling of total panic, being the woman who had cowered frantically in the flat, afraid to go out, and once out, afraid to return.

She drew a small sigh, one of gladness. At last she was free of it. The past six months had been a nightmare, but it was over. All that remained was a visit to St. Marcel, and then freedom. A new life; life as a single woman at an age when most girls were settling down to marriage. But first to find a place to stay for tonight . . .

Francesca moved away from the desk and reached for her case. A shadow materialised at her side, a hand reached for her arm without actually touching it. The action had the required effect. Francesca straightened up sharply, automatically drawing away from threatened contact. He was stuffing a number of documents into the inside pocket of his dark blue jacket. The desk clerk said something in French and the man put his hand out for a thick wad of brochures. He put them too into his pocket, had a further exchange with the clerk and then turned to Francesca again.

'I couldn't help overhearing your stuggle with the counter-clerk. Can I be of help?'

His tone was perfunctory, abrupt almost, but the sound of a true-blue English voice in the midst of a babble of French and German was sweet music to her ears.

She shook her head. 'I doubt it. Despite my non-existent French I did understand that there are no cars available until tomorrow.'

He put his head slightly to one side.

'Not touring alone surely?'

Francesca realised now that she had seen him before — on the flight from Paris. He had been sitting three rows behind her own and his presence had hardly registered at the time, for there was nothing to distinguish him from the other passengers. Brown hair, shorter than it was usually worn now, brown eyes, conventional suit, and facial features so ordinary that she doubted if she would recognise him if they were to meet tomorrow.

Now that he was standing next to her he was taller than she would have imagined and it seemed that the suit he wore covered an athletic frame. When she had passed his seat during the flight she remembered that he had idly glanced at her, pausing as he was about to drink from his glass. Momentarily his eyes had looked into hers and then he had looked away. Francesca had passed on, forgetting him almost immediately.

She looked away now from his cold, impersonal gaze, angry that she had noticed him at all, angry that he should think because she was English and alone she was a natural target for any man who might come along.

'I'm visiting.' She brushed a wisp of hair from her damp cheek. 'I caught an earlier flight than the one I'd intended. I was to have been collected at the original time but I sent a cable from Paris telling them not to bother sending transport. I thought it would be a simple matter to hire a car once I was here. Now I can hardly ask to be collected. It will take so long for someone to come, I may as well wait until tomorrow.'

He listened to her without interrupting, but his eyes had never left her face. 'Where are you going to?'

He was a stranger, asking questions, questions he had no right to ask. But they were both English in a foreign country, which somehow made the difference and she sensed he was used to asking questions, and having them answered.

'A little village called St. Marcel,' she answered, hoping that he might be able to recommend a hotel here in Bordeaux. With his command of the language it was certain that he was no stranger to the country.

'St. Marcel sur Dogne?'

She nodded. 'It's on a tributary of the Dordogne. Do you know it?'

'Yes, and I can help you. I'm going there myself, and,' he added, allowing himself a smile for the first time, 'I did arrange to hire a car before I left England.'

Francesca drew away, eyes downcast. 'Well, that's very kind of you, but . . . '

He needed no special powers to read her mind. He gave her the tight-lipped smile again. 'No strings attached, I promise you. This is just an offer to share my car. I'll have you in St. Marcel by late this afternoon. From what I heard before, I think the sooner you get to your destination the better. You don't seem very capable of looking after yourself.'

That was one statement she couldn't argue with.

She searched his face. His gaze was unwavering even though she knew he must consider her a singularly suspicious young woman. Suspicion came easily, even now. The only man she had entirely trusted in more than six months was Dr. Turner at the nursing home. As she looked into this man's face she suddenly felt that she could trust him too. The time had come to trust at last. It was her only salvation.

Her face crinkled into a sheepish grin. 'I'm sorry. It's become a habit to question . . .'

'Oh, I don't blame you,' he answered quickly. 'It pays to be suspicious of a man's intentions these days, or so I'm told. The art of giving for giving's sake is dying out.'

'Well,' she said briskly, 'this is a fortunate coincidence for me, Mr . . . ?'

'Devlin. Peter Devlin.'

She smiled again. 'I'd be glad to share your car, Mr. Devlin, if you'll allow me to share the expenses.'

'Definitely not. I'm going in your direction anyway. I'll be glad of the company for a while.'

'I really am very fortunate,' she answered, moving to take her case, but he was there before her.

'They're bringing the car round. It should be here by now.' He started towards the main door and Francesca followed. 'Did you want to eat first, or was that meal on the plane enough for you?'

'Oh yes, more than enough. I don't have a big appetite.'

A fleeting and perfunctory inspection of her, obviously confirmed her statement. She remembered days of abject terror when food, hunger, the bare necessities of living were forgotten.

'Oh, by the way my name is Francesca Varonne.' She gave a nervous laugh. 'We may as well have the formalities over.'

'I already know your name.' At the sight of her questioning look he glanced down at her suitcase tags.

'Oh, I see,' she murmured, feeling foolish.

When will I begin to be at ease again? she asked herself as they came out of the building.

In the full glare of the sun it was hotter out here than in the fraught atmosphere of the terminal building. She unbuttoned her coat, which had been armour against the cold June day she had left behind. She took a deep lungful of fresh air. After more than half a day spent in aircraft and airport buildings it was incredibly sweet.

'There she is!' Peter Devlin exclaimed, nodding in the direction of a cream-coloured Citroen.

She waited patiently while he put the cases into the boot. Then when they were in the car she waited while he tried out all the various levers and knobs.

He glanced at her as he checked with his map. 'It was your name that made me notice you,' he said and she answered with a murmured 'Oh.'

'With such a French-sounding name it seemed odd that you were having difficulty with the language. Miss Varonne sounds distinctly odd too.'

'If it must be anything it is Madame Varonne.' He looked at her again and she sensed his interest quicken. Automatically she fingered her wedding ring. 'I'm not French but my husband was, in a way.'

'Was?'

She looked straight ahead to where an errand boy on a bicycle with a basket full to overflowing was weaving a precarious way through the traffic.

'My husband was killed in a car accident six months ago.'

His eyes narrowed fractionally, painfully she thought. Was her own voice so bleak? she wondered.

Before he could speak she went on quickly, 'It would be best if you called me Francesca, even though it is an exotic name for such a prosaic creature as me.' She laughed although his expression hadn't altered. 'I'm not seeking confirmation of that statement, Mr. Devlin, or a denial. It happens to be true. My parents married late in life and by the time I was born they'd long given up hope of having a child. My name, I think, was the only bit of exotica they could give me. It belonged to an Italian woman they met during their honeymoon in Italy.' Her voice faltered under his unblinking scrutiny. He really was the oddest man. Her own reserve appeared warm against his.

'Please call me Francesca,' she said again as she looked away.

That request from a young attractive widow, alone in a foreign country with a compatriot might have sounded like an invitation, but coming from Francesca's lips it was no more than a cold formality.

Peter Devlin turned away from her, fired the ignition and concentrated on making his way through the traffic. Nothing was said for a while. Francesca stole occasional glances at his profile, an altogether unremarkable profile and quite unlike Paul's. Paul who had been handsome; so handsome that she marvelled at his love for her, whose looks could also be classed as unremarkable.

Paul. There was a lead weight around her heart. Paul, who had such a joyful love of life . . .

Peter Devlin was altogether a different man. Mysterious. He had caught her interest, which was something of an achievement, for nothing and no one had interested her in a long time. He was closed-in, she decided suddenly. He spoke, he smiled, but what was behind it she couldn't guess, for there was little enough warmth in his manner despite his outward gestures.

Strange she should notice that; she who was as cold as ice.

He had come to her rescue; what did it matter what kind of a man he was? He could be an escaped criminal for all she cared, as long as he got her to St. Marcel.

Guilt at her own thoughts made her

venture to speak again. She hated the silence. It seemed to hang heavily in the air.

'If anyone had offered me the use of a car just then I think I would have been overjoyed. Now I have not only the use of a car but someone to drive me so I can enjoy the scenery. How well things often turn out.'

He gave a laugh. 'When you were attempting to do battle with that clerk you were as white as a ghost. I thought you were about to explode at any moment. I've never seen anyone look so fierce.'

Her smile faltered. 'I was just angry with myself for not attending my French teacher at school,' she lied. 'Even though he spoke English well I'm convinced it's better to speak in a person's own language.'

'I must admit I've often found that to be true although it doesn't always work. Sometimes petty officials enjoy being awkward and take delight in demonstrating their power just for the heck of it.'

She turned in her seat so she could

look at him properly, turning her back on the endless vista of trees, hills, cliffs and tantalising glimpses of water. It was not as if she had come as a tourist.

'Have you been to central France before?' she asked with sudden interest.

'Yes, but slightly farther south than this. The last time, I passed through Perigord, liked it, and promised myself a stay when I had the chance.'

'And what decided you on such an out-of-the-way place as St. Marcel?'

'You did,' he answered frankly. She tensed slightly, withdrew a little, and he added, 'I'd made no special plans, purposely leaving my destination free. Your predicament decided me on my first port of call. I'd heard of St. Marcel, of course, and it's in the area I want to be in, so I decided to mix a little knight-errantry with fishing, sight-seeing, and all the rest.'

'Well, it's very kind of you,' she murmured.

'I'm glad to be of service.' A moment later he asked, 'What did you mean when you said your husband was 'in a way' French? With a name like Varonne he couldn't be anything else.'

She glanced listlessly out at the passing countryside. She registered that it was very beautiful as Paul had often described it, but Francesca saw nothing but green and undulating valleys, hills crawling with vines and towering cliffs. They made little impression on her.

'His parents were French. Paul's mother's the nervous type and she'd lost some relatives in the First World War. When she married Paul's father war was threatening again and it was affecting her nerves very badly, so Monsieur Varonne took her to England and got a job — he taught French in a boys' school.

'Paul was born in England; by the time the war was over he was at school and his father settled in his work. When he finished school and university his father died and his mother came back to St. Marcel to live with her brother-in-law and his wife.'

She looked at Peter Devlin's face, intent on his driving. 'Paul was very much an Englishman. He visited his mother and uncle often but he never considered coming here to live, or if he did he never mentioned it to me.'

'What sort of work did he do?'

'He worked for a firm that made engine parts. Paul travelled all over the world negotiating contracts. He was very successful at it. Usually, on his way back, he would visit St. Marcel; sometimes he called there first. That's what he was doing when he was killed — somewhere around here on one of these winding roads. His car went over a cliff. He was en route to Turkey this time. He never got there.'

There was a sudden silence.

'It doesn't hurt for ever,' he said and his voice was harsh as if it was an effort for him to speak at all. When Francesca looked at him she realised his voice had held its first vestige of warmth, although he had made an attempt to hide it.

'So I keep being told.'

She expected him to say something else; something sympathetic and was glad when he said instead, 'So you must know this area pretty well yourself.'

'No,' she answered with a broken little laugh. 'This is my first visit. As I said, Paul used to come at the end or the beginning of his business trips, so when it came to holidays we went elsewhere.' She added a moment later, 'Paul never encouraged me to want to come and I think it was because Madame Varonne never really liked me.'

'That's not an unusual situation, especially if he was an only son and his mother a widow.'

'I don't believe it was mere jealousy, because they were never that close, even before I met him. She came to London for the wedding and I think, because we were married in a registry office, she never came to think of us as being married at all. Like most Frenchwomen she's intensely religious, but Paul was like his father, so I'm told, and was

21

practically an atheist. He wanted nothing of a church wedding. I'm sure they argued about it, but Paul wouldn't give in.'

Francesca sat back. She had no idea why she was revealing so much to this stranger, a man who had no particular interest in her. Perhaps it was because he *was* a stranger and they were unlikely to meet again that she spoke so frankly. Whatever the reason for her new-found ability to talk, she was glad of it.

'And you?' he asked to her surprise. 'Or is that too personal a question on so short an acquaintance?'

His lips curved into a smile as if he had made a joke. If he had, Francesca felt she had missed the point of it.

'I wouldn't have minded a church wedding, but I must admit I didn't give it much thought; being married was the important thing.'

'It is to most women.'

She wondered how many marriage-minded females he had encountered. A man of, perhaps, thirty plus would have met many. Anyway it was not a question *she* was prepared to ask on so short an acquaintance.

To her surprise he stopped at the next village they came to. They had passed through several, all of them clustered around old châteaux or churches. Others were only names on signposts pointing up narrow lanes where they peered from heady heights over the surrounding verdant land.

Despite her protests he ordered coffee and sandwiches for her too at the only hostelry the village possessed, and with something akin to envy she watched his enjoyment of them. Because it would seem ungrateful if she did not, Francesca made a show of enjoying hers, and finally found that she did.

There was an endless supply of coffee from the eager proprietor and Francesca was amused at the groups of solemn-eyed children who had gathered around to watch them at their open air table. When she drew her eyes from them she found that Peter Devlin had finished his sandwiches and was sitting back in his chair watching her, something that caused her to fumble in her handbag for her cigarettes.

Before she could draw them out he was holding out a silver cigarette case. She was startled, more than a little surprised, for Paul, by whom she measured all men, had hated the habit in women.

With a murmured thanks she reached for one and as she did so she noticed an engraved inscription inside the case: *Love is for always. K.*

Francesca wondered who K was. She had told Peter Devlin a lot about herself in a short time, which was odd as she was not usually a forthcoming person, yet she knew nothing of him.

He lit his own cigarette and snapped out the flame. He returned the case and lighter to his pocket and she said, 'Do you usually enjoy this type of holiday? Most people I know make for the coast.'

'You'd be surprised how many people don't,' he answered, inhaling deeply.

'But I do have a seaside holiday coming up later in the year.' He smiled as if anticipating it with pleasure and then looked at her again. 'I decided to come to Perigord and let myself drift wherever it suited me.'

'Lucky for me.'

'I'm glad you think so.'

She finished what was left of her third cup of coffee and refused a fourth from the hovering proprietor.

'What do you do, Mr. Devlin, when you're not drifting around France?'

'I'm a Civil Servant,' he answered, finishing his coffee and crushing out his cigarette.

'Now you do surprise me,' she said, her own interest quickening.

It was so long since she had had any kind of an intelligent conversation with anyone. Peter Devlin, so far, had proved himself polite and kind, but no more, yet Francesca was enjoying his company. It was so different from silent sympathy, muttered and embarrassed phrases that meant nothing, and finally suspicious looks.

She sat forward, suddenly eager; to be interested, however mildly, in another was surely a sign of healing.

He looked up sharply. 'Why should it surprise you?'

She shrugged slightly. 'You don't look the desk type.'

'I do have one but I'm not chained to it.'

'Which department do you work in?' she asked doggedly, for she sensed that he didn't want to discuss his life. No doubt, being on holiday, he found her far more interesting.

'Home Office,' he answered, motioning the owner. He handed the delighted man some notes and pushed back his chair to the man's almost incoherent thanks.

As they walked towards the car Francesca glanced around her with interest at last. The brown stone buildings had hardly changed since the time they were built in the Middle Ages. It was all quite different to the home she had shared with Paul during their marriage. For the first time since leaving England she was glad she had come, not just for her own mixed-up reasons, but just for the joy of it and as a definite step towards the start of a new life.

'You're fortunate you can come and live in a lovely place like this,' he said as the village was left behind.

'I'm not,' she answered quickly and despite herself she shuddered. 'I mean I'm not coming here to live.'

She couldn't possibly stay. Her mother-in-law and the Varonnes would have to live in the family château, amidst ever-present memories of Paul, but Francesca knew her salvation lay in a new life, not the remnants of the old.

He glanced at her. 'You're going back?'

'I've put the flat in the hands of an agent, to dispose of it if he can while I'm away. He doesn't think there will be any difficulty finding another tenant. But I am going back,' she said, almost to herself, 'to get a smaller flat and a job. I just had to come this once. They wanted me to come and I couldn't refuse.'

He said nothing. He didn't need to. Just then the silence as she sat next to him was comforting.

2

As her companion had promised, they came to St. Marcel in the late afternoon. The village, like so many they had passed through, straggled down the hillside to the banks of the tributary, which ten miles hence flowed into the Dordogne.

St. Marcel had a central square, the hub of life in the village, and the château towered above it like the vigilant watchdog it had been over the centuries. Strange to think that suave, cosmopolitan Paul had been a direct descendant of those feudal landlords, often warlords. Inspired by such thoughts and seeing Paul's heritage for the first time, Francesca wished she'd had a child. Even though Chantal, Paul's cousin, would eventually marry, the name of Varonne would probably die out now. Coming from a family with no known roots in history, save for the roots which we all share, she considered it a shame.

However, it hadn't troubled Paul . . .

Peter Devlin said as they came into the square, 'There's a hotel over there. There's bound to be a room for the night.'

'If you have any trouble getting fixed up, I'm sure they'll give you a room up at the château. There must be dozens to spare, and after your kindness to me . . . '

He shook his head and put his foot down on the accelerator. 'St. Marcel is a little off the usual tourist route and it isn't the season yet. There'll be room.'

The car shot forward, frightening an old woman ambling along in front of them. She jumped out of the way and let forth a stream of invective. Francesca needed no translation to get the gist of it. Peter Devlin laughed, eased the car back up to her and pacified the woman with a few well-chosen words.

'I wish more than ever I'd listened to my French teacher when I was at school,' Francesca said when the satisfied woman had ambled off again. 'Oh, look, you don't have to take me all the way up the hill. I can walk quite easily from here and I'm sure you're longing to get settled with a room.'

'And I'm also longing to see this château of yours at close quarters. I've never actually met anyone who was going to stay in one. It must take an awful lot of upkeep. Quite a struggle I imagine.'

The road from the village to the château twisted tortuously upwards, although from below, its proximity had seemed much nearer. At each side of the narrow road elderly men and women toiled in the vineyards that still belonged to the Varonnes.

As they went higher Francesca caught glimpses of the red roofs of the village buildings and the shiny river snaking along the floor of the valley between woods and fields of ripening corn.

'Is it a famous wine?' he asked.

Francesca reluctantly returned her

attention to him. 'No. I believe it's casked and sent to Bordeaux where it's bottled under a collective name. What we would call 'vin du pays' I suppose. The sort the connoisseurs sneer at.'

The road ended when it seemed it could go no further without being lost in the clouds, although Francesca knew that by many standards the hill was not very high.

The car swept through a crumbling archway, one that once supported the gates to the château. They had gone long ago. From such close quarters the château looked enormous with its two lanterned towers and countless tall square windows.

There was a large paved terrace to the front of the château and it was onto this that the car drew. The moment it stopped Francesca got out, no longer wary of the doubts that had tormented her since the outset of her journey. She had never seen such a building, and the thought of being linked to it by her marriage to Paul was as heady as the view from the terrace.

She crossed to the edge and looked down. Below the road snaked down the hillside, a ribbon of grey amidst the brilliant green of the vines, and the red roofs of the village. Further away the river glistened, reptile-like, in the evening sun.

When she turned again Peter was frowning at her and she realised she had been smiling with pure pleasure for the first time since their meeting.

Immediately he looked towards the château, his hands on his hips, and Francesca's eyes followed the direction of his gaze. The walls were luxuriously dressed with ivy which crept between the ancient stones. The place looked so deserted it was hard to believe that successive families had lived here over the centuries.

Peter turned to her again and grinned. 'They didn't need a moat or a drawbridge, did they? With this view of the area they could have a nice handy trap ready and the oil nicely on the boil before the enemy was halfway up the hill. That's assuming, of course, that any potential foe still had enough breath left to fight.'

Francesca laughed and walked back to him. Now it was time to say goodbye she was oddly reluctant to see him go. As she glanced at the uncompromising façade of the château she realised that, perhaps, it was not so odd; the château was far from welcoming in its appearance. She'd had a letter, of course. A letter that was warm in its invitation, but it had come from Berthe Varonne, Paul's aunt, and not his mother.

She smiled at him shyly, for despite five years of marriage to outgoing, extrovert Paul, she had retained her inherent shyness. She was wondering just what to say to him when one half of the thick, studded door swung open.

Both Francesca's and Peter's attention was diverted by the appearance of a woman who gasped and ran down the steps the moment she saw them. Automatically Francesca went to meet her. Her hair was a dark helmet, streaked with grey, her body dumpy but streamlined somewhat by the simple wool dress she wore.

'You must be Berthe,' murmured Francesca shyly.

The woman gave her a strained smile and looked her over quite deliberately. Then she said, 'So you are Francesca. *Ma chére* Francesca. You have come. Welcome.'

She embraced Francesca loosely, bestowing a cool kiss on her cheek. Over Francesca's shoulder she looked at Peter Devlin and turned her worried gaze back to the girl, questioning her silently.

'This is Peter Devlin, Berthe,' Francesca explained as she drew away, sensing Berthe Varonne's silent disapproval. 'He was kind enough to give me a lift from Bordeaux, otherwise I wouldn't have been able to get here until tomorrow. There wasn't a car to be had until then.'

'You are most kind, monsieur,' said Berthe Varonne. Her voice was cold and

Francesca was surprised at the chilling welcome she gave this man who had been more than kind to her.

However, Peter Devlin seemed not to notice. 'It was a pleasure,' he answered formally and then proceeded to take her suitcase out of the boot of the car.

Berthe Varonne put her arm around Francesca's waist and led her towards the house. 'You're so thin,' she chided, glancing around uneasily. 'And we were worried about you when we received your cablegram. We weren't quite sure what to do about meeting you.'

Three wide shallow steps led up to the door. Above it, carved in the stone and unmarred by the strangling ivy, was the ancient coat of arms of the Varonnes — a phoenix rising from the ashes.

Francesca paused, gazing at it transfixed; Paul always wore a gold medallion around his neck and it bore that same crest.

Berthe Varonne kept her hold on Francesca and hurried her into the enormous flagged hall. The walls were stone too and, except for a shield facing the door, were unadorned. Bleak and cheerless, the only light that entered was through the partially open door and two windows high up in the walls which shed narrow shafts of sunlight onto the floor.

Paul's aunt looked at Francesca and smiled. Francesca, half-heartedly, smiled back. Peter followed them in and Francesca could have laughed at his expression of awe and dismay, for it almost exactly mirrored her own on entering.

He looked at her quizzically and she felt she could read his mind. 'Do people actually live here?' he was asking himself. It gave Francesca a sense of camaraderie which cheered her. It needed to. This place was as cheerless as a tomb.

'Thank you so much, Mr. Devlin,' said Berthe Varonne before Francesca could speak. 'This is so kind of you.'

Her voice was not overloud, yet it echoed around the walls. She had hurried over to him, hardly allowing him to enter and her voice was filled with a hearty warmth that was so much at odds with her otherwise reserved manner.

He said, 'Goodbye, Francesca,' and she had hardly echoed, 'Goodbye,' before the great studded oak door had closed behind him. It had the awful sound of finality, like the closing of the door to a prison cell, and its closure darkened the hall even further.

Francesca turned to Paul's aunt, horrified. 'I didn't thank him properly, Berthe.'

Berthe Varonne smiled, but tightly again. 'Of course you did, my dear. I am sure Mr. Devlin only wants to be away now he's delivered you safely. You have brought him out of his way, remember. We must not force him to stay just out of politeness.'

Francesca felt, a little sadly, that what Berthe had said was probably true. 'But he may not be able to find a room . . . '

Berthe Varonne began to lead an

unwilling Francesca towards the great stone stairway. 'You need not worry. I was speaking to Pasquale only yesterday — he owns the hotel — and he was complaining very bitterly at the lack of guests at the moment. Of course it is due to the cool spring we have had. The harvest will be at least two weeks delayed, if not more,' she went on breathlessly. 'Now it is warmer it will be busier for us all. Poor Pasquale was quite excited at the prospect of having an English guest so early in the season.'

Francesca looked at the woman sharply. 'What English guest?'

'Mr. Devlin. Why else would he have brought you here if he wasn't staying? There couldn't be two Englishmen coming to St. Marcel with the same name. So, you see, my dear, you need have no fear for your friend.'

Francesca automatically followed Madame Varonne up the stairs. The stone baluster rail was cold to her touch. She was sure Peter Devlin had told her he hadn't planned to come to

St. Marcel, yet no longer could she trust her own ears. At the beginning of the journey she had hardly been attentive.

'Have you known Mr. Devlin long?' Aunt Berthe asked.

Francesca peered around. Cold grey stone, unrelieved by paint or carpet, was everywhere. Ahead of them on the landing was an old tapestry depicting the Varonne phoenix.

She gave her attention back to Paul's aunt who had paused before her and was looking at her intently. Her small dark eyes had a glittering intensity as she waited for a reply to her question.

'I don't know him at all,' Francesca answered.

It was true and she regretted it. What is more, Berthe Varonne knew she regretted it. Francesca wondered if the woman resented her even speaking to a man, perhaps even suspected her of a liaison. As if she would while visiting Paul's home. Was Berthe Varonne outraged because she had arrived in the company of a man? Francesca wondered. Was that behind her cool, tight smile and her nervous way of talking?

'We met at Bordeaux, as I told you. He overheard my effort to hire a car and kindly offered to bring me himself as he was coming this way. That is why . . . '

Berthe Varonne's eyebrows rose a shade. 'So you did not know him before?'

'No, no, of course not. I told you; we met at Bordeaux for the first time this morning. I'm very grateful to him. He saved me a great deal of trouble.'

'It was very convenient,' Berthe said thoughtfully, still staring at Francesca. 'Very convenient indeed.'

Francesca suddenly wanted no more talk of Peter Devlin. She brushed past Berthe and said, a little breathlessly, aware that she had left the enquiry a little late. 'How is Maman? May I see her now?'

Berthe Varonne's face seemed to crumple. She climbed the rest of the stairs like an old woman, clinging to the baluster rail for support.

'Ah, poor Marguerite. It is tragic.'

They had reached the upper hall. Francesca stood, bathed in the sunlight that was streaming through an upper window. She was glad of it, glad of the warmth that was disposing the chill which had crept into her bones when she had entered the château.

'Maman is ill?'

Berthe Varonne sighed. 'Nothing more than is expected. She worshipped Paul, simply worshipped him.' She looked at Francesca and then her glance slipped away again. 'I think it only fair to warn you that she hasn't accepted Paul's death. Her mind has, how do you say? refused to accept it. She still believes he is alive. Finally the doctor decided she will never accept the truth and it is kinder to go along with her and pretend too. It is heartbreaking for us too. The doctor called this morning. The excitement of your coming, I think, was a little too much for her. She had to have a sedative, so I am afraid you will not be able to see her today.'

Francesca tried hard not to let her relief show to this woman.

Berthe gripped Francesca's hand and Francesca stared down at their two hands. 'Please, Francesca, when you see her you will go along with it too, won't you?'

Francesca shivered. An icy blast chilled her again even though she still stood in the shaft of sunlight. The hairs at the back of her neck prickled.

Suddenly Berthe Varonne stepped back and let go of her hand. 'Ah, here is Chantal. She is back from the village, and early too. She has been longing to meet you.'

Francesca turned round. The icy blast had come from a door at the end of the corridor. The light down there was too dim for her to see anything clearly, just a barely visible human shape. Chantal. Paul's cousin.

As Francesca turned, the door shut.

The draught had closed it with more force than was necessary.

Berthe Varonne touched Francesca's hand again as her daughter came towards them. 'My, how thin you are. We must concentrate on making you quite well again.'

'I am quite well,' Francesca contradicted. She didn't add, 'All I need to do is curb this absurd tendency to imagine things, like your unease now.'

'Chantal, isn't it wonderful to have Francesca with us at last? Now we are all together.'

Berthe Varonne beamed benevolently between her daughter and Francesca, but Francesca was looking at Chantal and experiencing a shock. Was this the little Chantal Paul had told her about?

She made a rapid calculation and realised that the little Chantal who had been thirteen years old when they were married was now a comely eighteen. A beautiful eighteen. Hair as black as a raven's wing cascaded down her back, and eyes as dark as bottomless pools regarded Francesca with interest but no warmth. There was no warmth anywhere in this place.

Francesca tried to inject some warmth into her own voice. She extended one hand which Chantal ignored, but not to be put off she said, 'I'm so happy to meet you, Chantal. Paul spoke of you often. I've always felt I've known you.'

'So you have come,' she answered, looking steadily at Francesca, ignoring her greeting completely. 'At last,' she added.

'You two will be the greatest friends,' her mother said, and to Francesca that statement seemed a shade too optimistic.

'Yes, we will be friends,' Chantal echoed. At last she drew her gaze away from Francesca and looked at her mother. She carried herself proudly; the Varonne blood in her veins and her looks ensured that she did. 'Maman, who was it I saw driving away from here just now? There was a strange man in a car.'

Berthe Varonne gave a little laugh

and stole a glance at Francesca before replying, 'Oh, that was an Englishman who was kind enough to bring Francesca from Bordeaux.'

Chantal looked at Francesca again. 'I didn't know you were bringing a friend with you.'

Francesca's own eyes grew hard as did her voice. 'Mr. Devlin is a gentleman I met at the airport this morning. He was kind enough to bring me as I had no other means of transport.'

How many more times must I repeat myself, she wondered angrily.

'Chantal,' her mother said quickly, 'you two will have lots of time to talk later. Just now I'm sure Francesca is very tired and would like a rest. I was just about to show her to her room . . .'

Chantal said nothing more; she just brushed past them and walked down the stairs, her hips swaying seductively beneath her tight skirt. She didn't look back, but the two women watched her go in silence.

At last Berthe drew her gaze away from her daughter. 'Ah, poor Chantal; she worshipped Paul too, since she was a little girl. His death was a great blow to her too.'

Everyone, it seemed, worshipped Paul.

Suddenly Francesca shivered as something touched her leg. She looked down and gasped in surprise as two narrowed eyes looked into hers. She stooped down and scooped up the cat into her arms.

'This cannot be Ninon!' she said, stroking the cat's silky fur.

'Yes, indeed it is. Our little Ninon. Chantal must have let her in when she opened the door. I put her out myself this morning.'

Ninon, the Siamese that Paul declared was never from his side when he was at the château. Poor little Ninon. Did she miss him too?

Francesca suddenly stiffened, paralysed by another nameless fear. She sniffed. It couldn't be, yet there could be no mistake. 'Who wears *Hombre*?' she asked sharply.

Berthe Varonne's eyes opened wide. She looked almost afraid. She thinks I'm raving, thought Francesca.

'*Hombre?* What is this *Hombre?*'

'It's an aftershave lotion. It has a very heavy perfume. Paul always bought some when he was in France because it's not available in England. I can smell it now.'

Berthe Varonne's eyes were still wide. She shrugged slightly, looking bewildered as she sought the answer. Suddenly she looked up and laughed. 'Many men come to the château to see Julien. Men from the wine syndicate in Bordeaux. It may even be Julien. He uses some kind of concoction on his face after his shave. Men do these days, but they never did when I was a girl. It was the women who wore the perfume.'

She positively beamed and went on quickly, 'I will tell you now, Francesca, where all the rooms are so you will not get lost.'

Where they stood on the landing the corridor branched into three. Madame

Varonne indicated the direction from which Chantal had come. 'Your room and Chantal's is down there. Along the corridor here is the living quarters; dining-room, sitting-room, and so on. My husband's study is on the ground floor, but that is the only room that is used downstairs. We cannot get staff as we used to do, and being only a small family it is more economical to live in a small part of the château.'

She waved her hand in the direction of the third corridor. 'Marguerite, Julien and I have our rooms down there. The corridor leads to the rest of the château but it was sealed off years ago. You will soon find your way around.' She gave her quick, nervous laugh again. 'It is not like the days of our ancestors when the whole château was in use.'

They began to walk down the corridor to the room Francesca had been allocated. Suddenly she had a desperate yearning to be alone, to be free of Berthe Varonne's uneasy presence. She still held onto Ninon as if the cat were a friend onto whom she must cling.

'Where was Chantal coming from?' she asked, glancing down the corridor, as Berthe paused to fumble with the door handle.

'That is an outside door. It is Chantal's own entrance from the terrace to her room.' She gave another of her uneasy laughs. 'Girls of eighteen are so independent these days. She insisted on her own private entrance. If I had made such a suggestion to my parents in my youth I would have had a whipping. But times have changed,' she added with a sigh. 'The steps go right up to the tower, but that is never used now.'

Francesca took a deep breath. The sweet, spicy smell was less evident now, almost non-existent, but she was sure it had been the same astringent Paul had used. Over five years she had become used to it clinging to Paul's clothes, her own, the air.

It was almost too heavy for a man.

Many times she had threatened, laughingly, to use it herself. She had never known another man who did, so encountering it almost as soon as she had entered the château was a weird coincidence.

Berthe Varonne eyed Francesca a little uneasily as she opened the door to a small rectangular room, furnished, if not luxuriously, then adequately. There was a single bed covered with a woven counterpane, a threadbare armchair, a scarred table, and a worn carpet that once might have had a vivid pattern.

Still holding Ninon, Francesca crossed to the window. It overlooked the terrace. The view more than made up for whatever else the room lacked.

'If you need anything which isn't already here, Francesca, please let me know.'

'Thank you. I will,' she answered, coming away from the window.

Berthe Varonne put out her hands to take the cat and although oddly reluctant to do so, Francesca relinquished her. The Siamese mewed her protest too.

Paul's aunt began to back out of the room. 'Chantal's room is just next door and the bathroom is across the corridor. I've made sure there is lots of hot water for you in case you want a bath.

'I'll send Jeanne up with your case — she's the maid. Ask her for anything you need, Francesca; we want you to be comfortable here.'

'Thank you, Berthe,' she answered obediently.

Berthe went, closing the door behind her and Francesca drew a sigh of relief. She hugged her arms around herself and looked around. The high ceiling and the walls were soot marked, the fireplace now empty.

'*We want you to be comfortable here . . .*'

Berthe Varonne's words echoed in her ears. As if she could ever be comfortable here. Every inch of this great château resounded with memories of Paul. Everyone who inhabited these walls still mourned him and always would. There was and never could be an escape. It was a living mausoleum to the memory of the last of the Varonnes.

And there was no real welcome here. Just cold, empty smiles coupled with words that meant nothing. That was all that was here.

3

For two days Francesca remained within the walls of the château. Any suggestion by her to go out was neatly sidetracked. Indeed, talk of any kind was uncomfortable.

'Why on earth did they ask me here?' she asked herself constantly. 'Was it because it's their duty to Paul's wife, because I have no relatives of my own?'

She doubted such generosity, sensing that they had none.

The morning after her arrival she had a fleeting interview with her mother-in-law.

Francesca had not seen her since her wedding day and her memory was of a slim, delicate woman, very vivacious and very French. She had changed little, except that her hair had grown more grey during the intervening years. She still managed to look frail and utterly feminine in her lace nightgown.

She was propped against several pillows in a gigantic four-poster which emphasised her frailty. She held out her arms in welcome and Francesca, uncertain still of her welcome, allowed herself to be clasped to a thin bosom and even managed to put a small kiss on that pale, dry cheek.

'You're here at last,' Marguerite Varonne beamed. 'I'm so sorry I was too tired to meet you last night. Berthe said it was the excitement and I suppose it was. I am not too well these days. But, then, I don't suppose you missed me when you were seeing my son after all these months . . . '

Francesca stiffened, although she had been warned, Berthe Varonne had remained in the room and flashed Francesca a warning look. Since she had arrived Berthe Varonne had never been far from her side.

Francesca sank down into a chair by the bed. It was going to be grotesque having these unreal conversations with her mother-in-law, painful too, but in this way she could help to alleviate, even prevent, such suffering coming Marguerite Varonne's way. Francesca envied her a little her dream world.

'I'm glad to be here. You musn't worry about last night; I was tired too.'

Marguerite Varonne leaned over and touched Francesca's hand. Despite her revulsion she let it remain there.

'I never remembered you being so pretty, Francesca. Your hair is quite beautiful. I think you've lost weight. It's your illness, of course. You'll soon put on weight while you're here. Madame Resaque is a wonderful cook, and the air here is so very beneficial.' Her face dimpled. 'And now we are all together, here at St. Marcel, and that is how it should be for the Varonnes.'

She beamed with pleasure at the thought and Francesca closed her eyes in anguish. *I'm not going to be able to bear it*, she told herself silently.

Berthe Varonne hurried forward. 'I think you have talked enough for the moment, Marguerite. You know the doctor says complete rest and no excitement for you. Come, Francesca, we have much to do.'

'But Berthe,' her sister-in-law complained, looking rather like a fractious child, 'Francesca has only just arrived . . . '

'Yes, and there will be more opportunities for you to talk. Francesca is not leaving here tomorrow, you know.'

If only I could, thought Francesca. My original reservations about coming here, the reluctance I felt at Bordeaux, were the right ones.

As Berthe spoke, Francesca was already on her feet, glad of the opportunity to go. A few minutes in Marguerite's company was more than enough.

She could bear them to talk of Paul; she wanted them to. After months of not talking of him she could bear that, but not this, not for long.

'Remember,' Berthe added briskly, 'Paul hasn't seen his wife for a long time. You must not monopolise her.'

It seemed that Berthe Varonne had

spoken the magic words. With good grace Marguerite was prepared to let Francesca go.

Outside the room Francesca waited while Paul's aunt closed the door. Then she looked, tight-lipped, at Francesca who was clenching and unclenching her hands without even realising she was doing it.

'I know this cannot be easy for you, nor is it easy for us, but it is good for her. That is what we must remember.'

Francesca nodded, knowing it to be true.

From the moment of her arrival Francesca was rarely alone. Mostly it was Berthe Varonne who kept her company, speaking almost constantly, mostly of nothing in particular, as if the silence troubled her.

Mealtimes were shared with Julien Varonne, Berthe's husband. He was a tall man, and dark as were all the Varonnes. He made an effort to be friendly, but Francesca, somehow, could not like him any more than she liked the other members of his family. He resembled Paul, but Paul had laughed a lot, had possessed warmth. Behind Julien's manner was pure ice.

It came as a relief to Francesca when she learned that Julien stayed out for most of the day attending his business matters. Francesca was not drawn to Berthe who seemed rarely to relax, but she preferred her company to Julien's.

Francesca made spasmodic attempts to court Chantal's friendship but the girl remained politely cold and as she was out of the château frequently it ceased to matter after a while.

And after two days Francesca realised she preferred her own company to that of any of the Varonnes, although she was rarely allowed to enjoy it.

She wondered how long she was expected to stay, how soon she could decently leave. Not for a while anyway. She only hoped that by the time she did leave she would not be reduced to a screaming madness by these oddly behaved people.

Even the two retainers, Jeanne and

Madame Resaque, were tight-lipped and uncommunicative, and hampered by her lack of knowledge of the language, it was impossible for Francesca to converse with them.

On the afternoon of the second day, she felt she had to go out. She had escaped to her room after lunch by pleading a headache and thus also escaped another meeting with Marguerite. She slipped on her coat and hurried down the corridor, unhesitatingly going towards the door Chantal used.

Francesca had no idea why she was acting so furtively; she only knew that it was somehow difficult to act normally in the château with one or other of the Varonnes always around her.

My imagination again, she chided herself. Why shouldn't they always be around? They live here.

She straightened her shoulders and told herself to stop creeping around. Nevertheless she turned the door knob carefully. The door opened on well-oiled hinges. Francesca closed it carefully behind her and found herself on a half-landing. Stone steps spiralled upwards to the tower room and downwards to the outside door.

As she hesitated there Ninon streaked down from the tower making Francesca gasp with fright. She relaxed again, laughing out loud at her own timidity.

She started down the stairs, following in Ninon's wake, but had only gone down two when she paused with breath held, listening. There had been a noise. It was only a faint noise but she was certain she had heard a footstep above on the steps to the unused tower room.

It seemed hours that she stood in frozen immobility, but in reality it was only seconds. She waited, ears straining for the sound of breathing, and it seemed that someone else was waiting and listening too.

'Jeanne,' whispered Francesca, irritated that she had whispered at all. 'Is anyone there?' she asked in a bolder voice.

The sound did not come again, if, indeed, there had been one at all.

Echoes of her own footsteps, she told herself.

She shivered, for the steep stairwell, because of its nature, was draughty. She hurried to the bottom without pausing again. She didn't want to start imagining things again, imagining people who weren't there. Madness lay in that direction.

To Francesca's relief the door at the bottom was unlocked. She had a sudden fear of having to return that way, knowing that nothing short of the door being locked would induce her to go back up those steps just then.

The door swung open letting in a blast of warm air and dazzling sunlight. Francesca hurried out, blinking momentarily at the harshness of the light after the dimness of the château. She was almost running when she gave a cry of alarm, for Chantal had come round the corner and almost bumped into her.

She stopped quite still, as did Francesca. The door slammed shut behind them in the draught.

'What are you doing here?' Chantal demanded.

'I was going for a walk,' Francesca replied, returning the bold stare. 'It was quicker for me to use this door than the main one. I assumed it wasn't for your exclusive use as it wasn't locked.'

'Where are you going?'

Francesca was beginning to be angry again. 'Just for a short stroll. I haven't been out for two days.'

Without a further word Chantal went past and into the château. Francesca watched her go. It was probable that there were few young men in St. Marcel whose hearts were not gladdened by the sight of those sensuous lips, or whose pulses weren't sent racing by the sight of the seductive swing of her hips.

Generations of aristocratic breeding had not diminished the sheer primitiveness of Chantal's allure.

Francesca frowned as the door slammed behind Chantal. Not at any time had she made an attempt to be friendly and Francesca wondered why.

Perhaps, like many beautiful women, she resented the presence of any likely rival. Francesca's lip curved into a grim smile; that could well be a joke.

She shrugged to herself, casting off all thoughts of Chantal, and walked slowly round to the front of the château, savouring the air as she went. As she turned the corner the breeze lifted her hair. It gave her a delicious feeling of freedom. She wanted to laugh out loud at the sheer joy of being alive on such a day. Surely, she thought, that must be healing at last.

As she passed through the ruined gateway she glanced back. The château looked deserted. Yet again Francesca marvelled at its close links with Paul; Paul who had loved contemporary furniture and art, who insisted on a flat with every modern convenience. Yet, being here at last, she couldn't deny that his presence was almost tangible in every stone of the building.

She had gone but a hundred yards, down the lane through tangled woods of oak and chestnut, when hurrying footsteps came up behind her. She stopped and turned, smiling to greet Julien Varonne. Francesca was hardly surprised that they'd sent someone to accompany her. She wasn't surprised at all.

Perhaps they had a code which forbade the neglect of visitors to the extent of being with them at all times. But she wasn't a visitor; she was Paul's widow. Now she was at St. Marcel she completed the complement of mourners and they were not letting her off lightly. Paul's widow she was. Paul's widow she must stay.

Or perhaps they thought her insane and in need of constant scrutiny.

Francesca brushed aside her unworthy thoughts. Wild imaginings again. She had been right the first time; they were over anxious not to neglect her.

'Julien,' she said, giving him a warm smile to make up for her dislike of him. 'How nice to see you. I had no idea you were home this afternoon.'

One thing she realised now; Julien did not wear *Hombre* after shave lotion.

He smiled with relief at such a warm reception. 'I am going to the vineyard,' he said when he came up to her. He was slightly breathless from hurrying. 'Would you like to come with me? You might find it interesting.'

'I'm sure I will,' she answered.

Julien Varonne fell into step beside her. 'Is your headache better?'

'Oh, much,' she replied smoothly, amazed at how easily untruths dripped off her tongue. 'I'm sure a little fresh air will rid me of it completely.'

He thrust his hands into the pockets of his trousers. 'What do you think of our country, Francesca?'

'I think it's very beautiful, although I haven't seen as much of it as I'd like just yet. I hope to rectify that soon.'

'Yes, you must. Berthe must show you around. I wish I could say Chantal would — that would be ideal — but she is at a very awkward age just now. Teenagers are difficult to understand.

'But you must not overtire yourself. It is not long since you were out of hospital.'

'A nursing home,' she corrected automatically.

'It is tragic about Marguerite, is it not? She has been like this since we broke the news of Paul's death.'

They had come to the slopes planted with vines. Among them the workers toiled, doing the tasks their forefathers had done for centuries before them — and for the same masters. One or two glanced at them idly, but none showed undue interest.

Francesca stopped and faced him squarely. 'It is tragic and I pity her, but I have no intention of becoming like that too. Paul is dead. Tragically and too young, but nevertheless dead. It's taken me a long time to gain the courage to face that unpleasant fact. He's dead,' she repeated, 'but we are alive. I am alive, and I have a future.'

There, he could believe she was hard-hearted. Paul had been the axis of her life too and his death had left her spinning in a void, but she meant what she had said; she would make a future for herself, somehow.

Julien Varonne's eyes softened with pity. It was so unexpected that her throat became tight and she could have easily cried.

'My poor child,' he said. 'My poor child.'

He drew his eyes away from her a moment later and, turning abruptly, he addressed an old man nearby. The old man replied to Julien's questions in a torrent of guttural French and, unable to understand even the gist of it, Francesca looked around her.

A girl was working nearby. Francesca noticed her because not many young people were working in the vineyards. Out of the mists of her own churning emotions Francesca was aware of the girl's eyes upon her face. Julien spoke to her next. The girl answered but as she did so she continued to look at Francesca. Francesca was only just aware of it, but there was a cold hatred in the girl's eyes.

Julien turned away. He gripped Francesca's arm. 'Eloise's brother has recently gone to Paris to study there. Paul made it possible before he died. It was arranged the last time he was here and I was just enquiring of Eloise his progress.'

They moved on. Julien was leading her away quickly. Francesca no longer knew, or cared, where she was going. Her own ferocity had shaken her. Apathy had gone. She realised she had taken the first steps towards living again and it was odd that it had happened at the place that was Paul's birthright.

★   ★   ★

'Did you find your tour of the vineyard interesting?' Berthe asked that evening over dinner.

They ate fresh river trout followed by steaks and the truffles for which the area was famous. The fresh air had given Francesca's appetite renewed vigour and she ate heartily for the first time in months. Marguerite was not present which eased the tension always present in Francesca when her mother-in-law was around.

Any form of mental aberration was embarrassing and Francesca was beginning to be more sympathetic towards the embarrassment suffered by her acquaintances during her own temporary spell of abnormality. The sight of Marguerite Varonne always elicited her silent thanks that she, herself, had come through virtually unscathed.

'It was extremely interesting,' she answered, hardly able to say that she had paid scant interest; that her only vivid memory was of a girl whose eyes flashed a furious hatred.

Francesca no longer considered it disquieting though. She had come to the reluctant conclusion that these people were dour and faintly hostile by nature.

The dining-room was not as big as

Francesca had expected. The original dining-room was on the ground floor, a big vaulted room capable of seating over a hundred people at once. This room was once one of the countless bedrooms before the château had surrendered to the advent of age and economy. The table at which they sat was the original, however, and it dwarfed the room. A huge refectory table, it had been carved from one solid piece of oak. Now it bore the scars of use by countless generations.

They ate from a Sèvres dinner service which was also old and precious as were the cut glass goblets in which the mediocre wine sparkled. In the past the Varonne treasures must have been something to see; now the little which remained was in constant use, probably as a reminder of the glory gone by.

'Is it possible for me to hire a car?' Francesca asked after a while. 'I'd like to explore a little of the area while I'm here. It's too good an opportunity to miss.'

Her tone was deceptively mild. She was, in fact, determined within reason to come and go as she pleased. She refused to be walled up on Paul's tomb. She had her memories. Heaven knew she needed nothing else to imprison her.

'A car?' echoed Berthe.

Her expression made Francesca smile involuntarily. She was reminded of the scene in *Oliver Twist* where the boy asked for more food. Francesca's request could hardly have elicited more astonishment.

Julien looked anxiously at his wife. Francesca could not help but wonder, rather maliciously, if she were outraging their sensibilities in not weeping into her handkerchief and wearing perpetual black. But she'd done enough of that. Yes, far too much.

Oddly enough it was Chantal who came to her rescue.

'Naturally, Maman,' she said easily, 'Francesca wishes to see some of our countryside. It will do her good to get out. It cannot be pleasant for her to stay here all the time, especially with Aunt Marguerite the way she is.'

Francesca looked at her in astonishment, distrustful of Chantal's motives, but Chantal's face bore an expression of innocence. Francesca decided that, perhaps, she had been a little too hard on Chantal without giving herself a chance to know her.

Even more surprising, Berthe smiled. 'Chantal is right. We have been too protective of you.'

'Protective?'

'Maman means because of your illness,' Chantal explained, 'and because of Paul . . . ' She bit her lip and Francesca felt a stirring of pity for the girl. She could understand her hero-worship of him. 'We are a little wary of driving on these roads. They can be treacherous as we know all too well.'

Chantal looked down at her plate. 'I appreciate your concern for me,' Francesca answered.

How stupid she'd been. How suspicious. It was only concern they felt;

quite a natural sentiment. She had wronged them.

'We have a car you can use,' offered Chantal. 'It isn't very smart — a small Fiat — but it is completely reliable. It should serve you well.' She looked at Julien. 'It will be all right for Francesca to use the Fiat, won't it, Papa?'

Her tone bore a slightly insolent quality, and it was as if the question were only a gesture to convention, meaning nothing. Chantal had offered the use of the car; Julien really had no say in the matter.

'Of course,' Julien murmured into his wine glass.

'That is very generous of you,' answered Francesca, still amazed. She looked to Berthe whose face had taken on a mask-like appearance. 'You really have no need to worry, Berthe,' she assured her. 'I'm quite well now. It was only shock after Paul's death that made me ill. And I'm considered a good driver. You don't have to be concerned on that score either. I shall be all right.'

A moment later she asked, 'Did the

accident happen near here?'

For a moment no one answered, then Julien looked at his wife, gave Francesca a small smile and said, 'About twenty miles from here. He was on business — for me. There is a château on a hill much steeper than this one. On every side there are cliffs. We know Paul transacted the business. Two minutes after he left, the car went over the cliff into the river.' He paused. 'We know that Paul was never the most cautious of drivers.'

Francesca glanced at Chantal in the silence that followed Julien's last words. The girl looked quite exotic in the flickering candlelight which Berthe insisted upon having in the dining-room. Her low cut dress revealed ample cleavage. All of Chantal's clothes seemed designed to show the most of her ripe figure.

Her dark eyes which looked into Francesca's were filled with an expression that Francesca could not entirely understand. As Chantal looked down to her plate again it seemed that she was enjoying some private joke.

4

The following morning Francesca collected the car from the converted coach-house that now served as a garage. It was flanked by two shiny models, but the Fiat's lack of smartness did not dismay Francesca; it represented freedom; an escape from the château and the tangible misery carried by each inhabitant.

The weather at St. Marcel had been consistently good since her arrival. The sun had never ceased to shine, although while she had been incarcerated in the château she might just as well not have been aware of it.

The car had no top, which was a testimonial to the constancy of good weather. For the first time she wore a summer dress, discarding the coat that had been like a protective shield around her whenever she ventured out.

Sunlight was often kind to blonde hair. It made Francesca's sparkle like spun silver. As she adjusted the driving mirror she caught sight of her own face. The ghastly pallor was already disappearing; spots of colour stained her cheeks and they were already losing their gaunt, haunted look. Soon her skin would darken into a healthy-looking tan.

As she backed the car out of the garage she expected someone — Berthe perhaps — to come running out of the château to join her. But no one came, and she gave a joyful wave as she drove through the gateway, should anyone have been watching from behind any one of those countless windows.

She drove slowly, getting the feel of the strange controls. It had been months since she'd driven, and this foreign car was so different to the ones she had used before, it was like learning all over again.

The workers were already busy amongst the vines and probably had been for hours now. No one took any notice of her, except the girl Julien had called Eloise. The girl paused in her work as Francesca approached, to stare at her with the same concentrated intensity that had been so disturbing before.

Impulsively, when the car drew level, Francesca stopped and leaned across the seat. 'Eloise,' she said, smiling confidently, '*Je m'appelle* Francesca Varonne . . . '

The girl had begun to walk away but when Francesca spoke she paused to look at her again. Her attitude puzzled Francesca, for Julien had said that Paul had helped her brother, and, in view of that, this hostility of manner was odd.

'You are Paul Varonne's wife,' she said in heavily accented English.

'Yes, I was. You speak English.'

'*Non. Je parle pas Anglais.*'

She stared at Francesca for a moment and the hardness in her eyes melted. The look that replaced it Francesca recognised well; she had seen it before, reflected in her own mirror, that look of haunting sadness.

Then the girl walked away, back along the orderly rows of vines where she began to speak loudly in rapid French to an older woman there, and it was as if she wanted to emphasise her last statement — that she could speak no English.

Francesca watched her go. The girl did not look back again. Then Francesca started up the car and let it roll slowly down the hill.

The girl did speak English; it was plain she just did not want to speak to her. She must, Francesca decided, try to understand these people. Perhaps she had been defying centuries of convention in trying to engage a worker in conversation.

These people had for generations literally belonged to the Varonnes, and, perhaps, were not always treated kindly by them. Now they worked and were paid fairly for their endeavours, but such inbred subservience and, perhaps, resentment, died hard. Francesca was a Varonne and those who worked in the fields were still serfs. She had seen the evidence yesterday when she was with Julien; she had seen the way they had remained silent until spoken to, answering Julien's questions respectfully, but volunteering nothing until then.

Staying at the château, amongst these people, it was very difficult to remember that she was living in the last half of the twentieth century.

The road twisted and descended steeply. Almost constantly Francesca kept her foot on the brake. She knew just where she was going now. There was one place she must visit before she could do anything, or go anywhere, else.

Francesca had seen the little church on her arrival at St. Marcel. She knew she must go there first, for someone was sure to ask if she had. Recalling her arrival she thought about Peter Devlin. The château itself and Paul's strange relatives had occupied her mind so fully for the past few days that only now did she think about the man who seemed so normal against this almost medieval back-drop.

Of course he would have gone by now. She felt a pang of regret at not having seen him again, although she hadn't expected to, and she was sure he would not have given her a second's thought after he had left her.

No one in the village seemed to have any respect for cars; they wandered in front of her heedlessly, so that she was forced to travel at walking pace. She could hardly help herself, as she crossed the square, from looking towards the small hotel. Tables shaded by umbrellas gave the grey, medieval frontage a garish look. Except for one of them, they were deserted at this hour of the morning. One hardy visitor was taking an early aperitif. Francesca was forced to stop the car to allow an ox-cart to cross her path. At any other time she would have taken in the quaint sight with interest, but now her attention was focused on the man outside the hotel. He wore dark glasses and was reading a newspaper. If he was aware of her scrutiny he did not betray it. He continued to read his newspaper unconcernedly and to sip at his drink at intervals.

Recollection tugged at her memory. She had seen him somewhere before, and recently, but the circumstances eluded her. Then she remembered. He was the Frenchman who had bumped into her at the airport. At the time she had hardly noticed him but his appearance must have registered automatically for her to remember him now.

There was little chance for Francesca to reflect on the coincidence of seeing him here before a car behind her hooted impatiently. The ox-cart had disappeared from sight. She let off the brake and drove out of the square.

The little romanesque church of St. Marcel stood halfway up the hill, past the village. Francesca parked outside, went round to the churchyard without bothering to go inside. A couple of minutes, she told herself; that is all it will take.

An old man was tending the narrow paths. Francesca smiled at him, asking hesitantly, '*Les Varonnes, s'il vous plait?*'

The old man nodded and waved his hand down the path. She continued down the path to its end. From there the Varonnes could still lord over the valley from their last resting place.

It was a huge granite tomb; the biggest of any there. Francesca steeled herself to read the tablets, silently thankful that there was no need to go inside.

There were several Paul Varonnes, but Francesca's eyes skimmed over their names. Paul's father had been brought back here after his death and his name was there too. Paul's grandfather, Paul Etienne. Francesca looked again, reading each one carefully this time.

She hurried back down the path. The

old man was still there. 'Paul Varonne,' she said. '*Je cherche, Paul Varonne.*'

The old man nodded again. '*Oui, madame. Les Varonnes.*' He waved again in the direction from which she had come.

'*Mon ami*, Paul Varonne. *Il est mort.*'

'*Oui, madame. Je suis desolé.*'

He turned back to his work and Francesca felt the familiar panic of total frustration mounting inside her. She didn't want his sympathy. She had assumed that Paul was buried in the family vault, yet there was no inscription on it.

The man picked up his basket into which he had been gathering weeds, and before Francesca could stop him he walked away. She let out a gasp of exasperation. 'Monsieur . . . ' she cried, but the old man did not hear, or did not heed.

Turning on her heel she ran out of the churchyard and flung herself into the car. She was trembling almost uncontrollably. Where was Paul? she asked herself, almost hysterically. If only she could have made the old man understand what she was looking for.

With deliberate slowness she took out a cigarette and lit it, and a moment later the shaking stopped. What a fool she was. Possibly in her nervousness she had missed it completely. She hadn't even gone around to the other side of the tomb. Yes, that was it. But she wouldn't go back, not today, not for anything.

She threw the cigarette out of the car and started up the engine. The desire to go anywhere had left her. She turned back towards the village. The man was no longer at the table. Perhaps it had been quite a different man to the one who had bumped into her in Bordeaux. Perhaps she hadn't seen him at all; he could have been a figment of her imagination just as all those other people had been; the ones who had haunted her life in London.

Francesca found she was trembling again just thinking about it. They had told her at the nursing home, that there was nothing more that could be done for her. She was cured. The future was up to her.

She stopped the car, parked it in a narrow alley off the square and walked towards the hotel. She sat down at one of the tables and immediately lit up another cigarette. This is becoming a bad habit, she told herself.

Almost immediately the waiter appeared and she ordered a brandy. The waiter returned quickly with a large measure. She drank it down in one gulp and sat back with her cigarette to allow it to have its famed calming effect.

Most of the village shops were in this square. Next door to the hotel was the *boulangerie*, its windows filled with crispy loaves and mouth-watering gateaux. The old women, busy with their shopping, wore the habitual black of the peasants despite the heat of the day. Only the younger women wore gaily-coloured frocks. Francesca doubted if the scene before her had changed much over the centuries except for the gradual replacement of motor vehicles over the traditional ox-cart which still persisted as a means of transport.

A shadow materialised at her side. She started, stifled a gasp and looked up.

'Hello, Francesca,' he said as he sat down opposite to her without waiting to be asked.

'Peter!'

She was quite unprepared for the joy she felt at the unexpectedness of seeing him. Her imagination had put him far away from St. Marcel by now.

He put his camera, sunglasses and a wad of picture postcards down on the table. He was so far removed from the château and its inhabitants, just a tourist who was unaware of her conflicts and fears. His presence was so reassuring that it took a great deal of self-control for her not to reach out and grasp those lean brown fingers from the sheer pleasure of seeing him.

'How are you, Francesca? Settling in at the château?'

'Oh, yes, certainly.'

The first rush of pleasure at seeing him was over. She looked away, embarrassed now at her own over-worked emotions.

'I'm glad to hear it. You looked a little upset when I first caught sight of you from across the square.'

He was watching her carefully. It was odd that he should have noticed, for she would never have considered him to be so sensitive to others, and that again was reassuring.

He ordered a coffee for himself and, without asking, one for her when the waiter appeared. Immediately he turned back to her and she knew she would have to answer.

'I suppose I was a little upset,' she agreed at last. 'But it's my own fault.' She gave a mirthless little laugh, keeping her eyes on the empty glass before her. 'I've been doing battle with the language again.'

'Oh,' he said slowly. 'Finding it hard to be understood again?'

She nodded. 'I went to see where Paul was buried this morning. I found the family tomb easily enough but not his name on it. There was a sexton in the churchyard, but he kept on nodding and pointing to the Varonne tomb. I tried to explain which Paul Varonne I was looking for, but it was useless. It was like taking part in a pantomime. There are several Paul Varonnes but not mine. I'm afraid I got rather upset . . . '

Peter Devlin frowned. The waiter brought their coffees and he paid for them.

'Would you like me to come and find out for you?'

She looked up at him at last. 'That's very kind of you, but there's no need. I'll just ask Berthe where it is, although when I left I realised I should have looked round the other side. It's probably there, only . . . well, I'm given to being impulsive. My calm is easily ruffled.'

He didn't press the matter, much to her relief. Even in his company nothing would induce her to go back to the church today.

'You've had a rough few months of it, so it isn't surprising.' She said nothing and, after tentatively sipping at his coffee and adding more sugar, he said, 'I've been hoping to see you. Will you have lunch with me today. Do drink your coffee before it gets cold.'

She seized on the cup gratefully. Lunch with him. Yes, she would like that. But she could imagine the effect it would have on the Varonnes. Only six months widowed and lunching with A Man. It wouldn't do. She must be entombed for ever with all the other Varonnes. Once a Varonne, always a Varonne . . .

Stop it, she told herself. Stop it!

Anyway Peter Devlin pitied her. She could tell. She wanted pity from no man.

'I can't. I think the Varonnes expect me back for lunch today.'

'Dinner then?' She shook her head. 'Another day?' She didn't answer and he asked, 'How do you find them?'

She could not help but reply, 'Oppressive,' but she added quickly, 'They took it very hard, naturally; my mother-in-law hasn't been very well since and sometimes the atmosphere gets a little heavy.'

He glanced up towards the château. 'It looks very interesting from here. I was hoping it was open to the public, but unfortunately it isn't.'

He looked back at her. Francesca stared into the depths of her cup. He was angling for an invitation. Instinctively she knew she couldn't issue one. He would be no more welcome than the first time he had come.

She said, 'There's little to see inside. A small part of the main building is in use for the family but the rest is closed off nowadays. They have no use for dozens of rooms and if there were works of art there once, there are few left. The vineyard brings in an income but I rather suspect it's an uphill struggle to make ends meet, as you suggested the day we arrived. You'd be terribly disappointed.'

'It must be a haven for children. All those disused rooms to play hide and seek in. How I would have loved it as a child. I still would, now I come to think of it.'

'There are no children at the château and when Paul was a child there was a war on so he never managed to visit until he was almost grown up.'

'Pity,' Peter murmured, and Francesca was disappointed in him. He was not the kind of man to utter banalities but, it seemed, they no longer had anything to say to each other.

'Another coffee?' he asked a moment later.

She shook her head. Instinct told her it was time to leave him. All that could be said, had been said, yet she was reluctant to go.

He glanced up at the château again. 'I've been making enquiries about that place,' he told her and she started slightly.

'Enquiries?'

'I always do. I'm fascinated by old buildings and their histories. This one, it seems, has quite a reputation. Apparently the Varonnes are an old and respected family but, as gossip has it, with several skeletons in their cupboards. The locals depend on the Varonnes for much of their livelihood but the family are not particularly liked.

'I was speaking to one of the waiters at the hotel, mentioning my meeting with you. His family go back as far as your late husband's, and tales get handed down.'

She said nothing and he went on, 'It's believed that each generation has turned up some kind of a black sheep. It all started when one of the Varonnes raped a beautiful gypsy girl who would have nothing of him. She jumped from the battlements of the castle that was here then, and as she jumped she put a curse on the Varonnes; she said that every generation would be dishonoured and the end of the family would be brought about by a gypsy.'

Francesca stared at him in amazement and then let out a harsh laugh. 'How ridiculous!'

Peter grinned. 'Yes, isn't it? But fascinating, you must agree. So far it has come true in some ways.' He lowered his voice a little. 'It seems, Francesca, that your father-in-law wasn't very well thought of around here. He was believed to have had communist leanings which discredited him with his father, and it was *his* cowardice when war was imminent that made him run to England. Your mother-in-law was of an old local family too, and as proud of being a Varonne as if she were born one. She didn't want to leave.'

He sat back in his chair and Francesca eyed him steadily. 'It can hardly matter now, can it? And if having communist sympathies and not wanting to be involved in a war is reason for being a 'black sheep' then I imagine it has been easy to find one in each generation.'

'Well, there's little the Varonnes haven't turned their hand to over the years, from abducting young girls, mysterious disappearances and a murder or two; oh, you know the sort of thing.'

'Yes, I do,' she answered calmly, sitting back in her chair. 'It's quite usual in old families, and none of the tales lose in the telling over a few hundred years.'

'I couldn't agree more. It's usually the sort of story that's told and embellished for the benefit of poor gullible tourists like me. It makes for a good story to be recounted over dinner back home though.

'There's another piece of information my garrulous waiter-friend told me, bringing the story nearer still; Paul's grandfather was thought to have been a collaborator during the last war.'

Francesca laughed harshly. 'The Varonnes just can't win, can they? Father a suspected Nazi, the son a suspected communist. It must be hard for a Varonne to do anything right according to the locals.'

Suddenly she sat up, linking her hands on the table in front of her. They were steady. She wanted no more talk of Paul's family. Deliberately she said, 'I was surprised to see you still here, Peter. I thought you'd have left days ago.'

He grinned. 'I could hardly go without saying goodbye to you, could I now?'

She flushed slightly at the recollection of the way he had been unceremoniously hurried out of the château by Berthe.

He propped his chin on one hand and regarded her steadily for a moment. 'Now, I've embarrassed you.'

She began to murmur a denial but he went on quickly, 'As a matter of fact, Francesca, this village suits me admirably. I have no intention of moving on.' She eyed him doubtfully. 'It was just what I was looking for after all although I didn't know it until I arrived with you.'

'But I was given to understand that you had already booked in at the hotel,' she said casually. He looked bewildered and she went on to explain. 'My aunt — Paul's aunt — told me that you were already booked in.'

His expression of bewilderment disappeared. 'Of course,' he said with a smile. 'There was an Englishman booked in the day before we came. The name, I believe, was . . . ' he hesitated a moment and then smiled, 'It was Denman. I expect it sounds the same to the French, just as their names sound very much alike to us.

'I meant what I said; I really like it here and I have you to thank for bringing me.'

She laughed. 'But it was you who brought me.'

'Not really,' he grinned. 'In some of the larger towns I get no chance to speak French with the inhabitants, and that I don't like. From here I can reach any place in the area quite easily. And to be sordid,' he added in a lower tone, inclining his head conspiratorially, 'the rates this hotel charge are ridiculously low. And for a few extra francs I've been able to hire fishing tackle for the day. I spent the whole of yesterday trout fishing.'

'Were you successful?'

His face crumpled into a wry grin. 'I'm afraid not, but I managed to have a good sleep. If anything came near to the bait it had plenty of time to get away again before I woke up.'

She laughed again. Was it really her laughter? It was such a strange sound.

'That's better,' he said, gazing at her in satisfaction. 'That really is much better, Francesca.'

She was suddenly very self-conscious. 'Have I looked so grim?' she asked.

'I reckon you're entitled to.' A moment later he glanced across the square. 'Well, here comes Chantal.'

Sure enough it was Chantal. With her unmistakably provocative walk she was making her way towards them.

Francesca was horrified. Not now, she thought. Not Chantal.

'You know Chantal?' she asked,

transferring her horrified gaze to him.

Peter's eyes were still on the approaching girl. Chantal was wearing a tight skirt and a low cut sweater. His lips curved into a smile. 'I gather most people know Chantal.' He looked at Francesca. 'I met her two nights ago. The hotel is the only meeting place around here — the only place there's dancing, I mean. Chantal is one of the regulars. She's quite a girl.'

Francesca's desolation was like a heavy weight upon her. So this was his reason for staying; the reason why he had been in the village square this morning. Chantal.

He got to his feet as the girl approached. She embraced them both with a smile, but her eyes lingered with pleasure on Peter. 'Hello. What a nice surprise. I hope I am not intruding on anything.'

'Your presence could never be an intrusion, Chantal,' he said gallantly as he held out a chair for her. 'What will you have to drink, or is it too early for you?'

'Oh,' she laughed, 'it is never too early. I would like a Pernod, if you please, Peter.'

Francesca felt herself fading into nothingness in Chantal's vivid shadow. She watched the girl covertly; the little mannerisms with him, the familiarities, and the way her eyes held his provocatively. Then she said something to him in rapid French. Francesca was only able to catch 'chéri'.

Peter answered her, also in French, and then, looking amused, he glanced at Francesca. 'I think we'd better speak English, Chantal. Francesca, remember, can't understand what we're saying otherwise, and it would be rude.'

Chantal sat back and smiled. The waiter appeared with the Pernod and as he placed it in front of Chantal she flashed him a smile that almost caused him to knock it over.

Then she looked across at Francesca. 'Yes, I forget. I was rude and I am very sorry, Francesca.'

Francesca, however, was in no doubt

that Chantal had deliberately tried to exclude her from the conversation. There was no need, for she felt excluded already. Whatever language they spoke, it was to each other.

Chantal gave her a malicious grin. 'Amazing, is it not? Francesca was married to a Frenchman and yet she cannot speak our language.'

'I never had to,' Francesca retorted. 'Paul spoke English as well as I do. He only spoke French when he was here, so there was no need for me to learn.'

Chantal turned back to Peter who had been looking amused at the obvious antipathy between the two. 'We were so grateful when you brought Francesca to us, Peter.' She glanced at Francesca fleetingly and then back to him, resting her hand on his. 'Papa wanted to go to London to collect her himself but with business commitments it was impossible. It was a worry to us because poor Francesca had been so ill, but she is looking much better now, don't you agree?'

Francesca looked down at the table. She hated being witness to such an obvious flirtation. She didn't care how many liaisons Chantal had, with countless men, but she desperately wished Peter Devlin was the one man to resist such overtures. But Peter Devlin *was* a man and there could be few who would withstand Chantal. They had met days ago, so for all Francesca knew, aware of Chantal's nature they might be lovers already.

'I think she looks fine,' Peter answered.

Chantal sipped appreciatively at her drink, pausing frequently to smile at the man at her side. 'I have been talking to Maman. She would like you to come for dinner soon. Say you will, Peter. You're not thinking of leaving soon, are you?'

'No,' he answered thoughtfully. 'As I was just mentioning to Francesca before you arrived, I like it very much here and I think I'd like to stay a little longer.'

'*Là*,' she said brightly, 'then it will be arranged.' She glanced at Francesca's stony face, looking amused. '*Chère* Francesca, it is time we returned for lunch. You look as if you are exhausted and that will never do. We do not want you to have a relapse while you are staying with us.'

Francesca needed no further encouragement. She scrambled to her feet, gathering up her bag and keys clumsily. Without looking up she said, 'Goodbye, Peter. Thanks for the coffee.'

She left Chantal to say goodbye to him in whatever way she wished. It didn't take her long, for the girl joined her in the car almost immediately. Francesca said nothing, aware that Chantal's face wore a complacent smile. Perhaps they had just arranged to meet tonight, Francesca thought, and she was furious with herself for letting it matter.

The car swept into the square. Out of the corner of her eye Francesca saw that Peter was still sitting at the table.

He raised his hand in salute as they passed. Francesca ignored him but Chantal giggled and blew him a kiss. Then she turned her mocking gaze on Francesca.

'So that is why you were so anxious to go out alone. What a dark horse you are, Francesca.'

A little gasp escaped Francesca's lips. 'Don't be ridiculous, Chantal. I never expected to see Peter today. An accidental meeting in the square hardly amounts to a secret liaison.'

'But nevertheless, you were glad you did see him, isn't that so?'

'I think I know what you're hinting, Chantal, and you are talking rubbish.'

Chantal was quite unperturbed. 'No, it is not,' she answered blandly.

'You will learn, Chantal, as you grow older, that a man and a woman can meet and be friends and nothing more.'

Chantal laughed. 'Who are you trying to fool; me or yourself?'

'What business is it of yours who I meet anyway?'

'You will learn, Francesca, that what concerns one Varonne concerns us all.' She threw her head back, turning up her face to the sun. 'I understand you far better than you understand yourself. You pretend that Paul has left you heartbroken but already you are seeking his successor.'

If Francesca hadn't been driving she would have slapped Chantal's face. 'You're accusing me of possessing your own meagre standards of behaviour,' she said through clenched teeth. What was it about this girl that had the power to get beneath her skin and irritate?

Chantal turned to look at her again. 'You English are strange; you are ashamed to admit your feelings. Are you always so cold and controlled? Paul couldn't have found you so. I knew him. He was every inch a Frenchman, and knowing him as I did, I cannot understand how he could have married you . . . '

Francesca shot her a furious look. She broke off, biting her lip. 'I see more than ordinary people. I am part gypsy, you know,' she added a moment later.

At that Francesca had to laugh. 'Oh, Chantal, really!'

Chantal's dark eyes narrowed furiously. 'Julien is not my father,' she snapped. Francesca's laughter died and Chantal knew she had scored. 'My parents were married for many years and there were no children. One summer some gypsies came to St. Marcel . . .'

'Gypsies!' gasped Francesca, suddenly remembering Peter's story of the gypsy's curse. She had laughed at the absurdity of it but beneath her laughter lay unease.

'Are you shocked, Francesca?' Chantal mocked. 'My mother fell in love with one of the gypsies. He was very handsome.' She began to laugh. 'So the last of the Varonnes is not a Varonne at all.'

'Does Julien know of this?'

'I expect so, although of course we have not discussed it. I imagine my mother has though. The gypsies returned year after year and my father with them. I remember him well. Julien doesn't mind as long as the knowledge is kept within the château walls.' She smiled again. 'I can tell you though; you are family, Francesca.'

Francesca changed into a lower gear as the car laboured up the hill. The workers were sitting beneath shady trees eating their lunch.

'Why does the girl called Eloise look so hostile?' she asked as they passed countless pairs of blankly staring eyes.

Chantal rested her arm along the back of the seat. 'Why do you think she is hostile?'

'That is what I am asking you,' Francesca snapped, growing heartily sick of the girl's sly innuendoes. Chantal was trying to inject a hidden meaning into everything she said and Francesca had the feeling she was being laughed at.

Chantal shrugged. 'They are proud, these people. They are poor too. They accept our help because elsewhere they would get none, but they are still proud enough to resent it.'

If Francesca expected some dramatic revelation she was disappointed. Peter's voice, talking of abductions and murder, was still loud in her ears; food for an active imagination such as hers.

'Where were you going if not to meet Peter?' Chantal asked as they swept through the ruined archway. From her tone it was plain that she was still not entirely convinced.

'I went to see the grave . . . Paul . . . '

Francesca stopped the Fiat outside the garage. 'Yes, of course. You are the dutiful widow, are you not, Francesca?'

Francesca looked at her sharply. Chantal was remarkably shrewd. Francesca could readily believe her gypsy blood.

'I couldn't find it — him.'

'Naturally. You would have done better to ask first. Aunt Marguerite goes there often. It was decided not to inscribe his name yet.'

Francesca sighed. She should have

known. She had almost been reduced to hysteria too.

Her head was bowed over the steering wheel. 'And I thought . . . for one moment, I thought . . . '

'Yes, what did you think?' asked Chantal in a very soft voice.

Francesca looked at her, brushing away a wisp of hair that had blown in front of her eyes. 'I thought . . . it was crazy I know . . . but I thought, perhaps, he'd committed suicide and no one dare tell me.'

Chantal smiled. 'Didn't you know him better than that?'

Francesca nodded. 'There is something else you should know though, Francesca,' said Chantal a moment later and as Francesca looked up at her her lips curved into a cruel smile. 'Maman warned me not to tell you — Paul is not there.'

'Not there . . . ?'

'His car plunged off a high cliff into the river. It was particularly deep at that point and he was never found. The police believe his body was drawn downstream and became lodged under a rock somewhere. It is doubtful he will ever be found.'

'*Please*, Chantal,' Francesca begged, closing her eyes tightly.

'I'm sorry, but I think you have a right to know. You are not a child. You were his wife. Now they will be angry with me for telling you, but I don't care. Paul cosseted you like a small child, but I don't see why we should too.'

Chantal opened the door and slipped out of the car. When she had closed it again she leaned on it negligently. 'Do you miss Paul, Francesca?' she asked.

For a moment Francesca was shocked into silence. In Chantal's face she saw nothing but curiosity. 'Of course I miss him,' she answered, looking away quickly.

Chantal's lips curved into a smile. 'Of course,' she mocked. 'I've told you I have remarkable powers.' She gave a little laugh. 'You cannot fool me as easily as the others.' She tossed back her luxuriant mane of inky-black hair. 'Paul and I were very close . . . '

'Yes,' she answered dully, refusing to rise to Chantal's childish taunts. Chantal was jealous, she realised it at last. She had loved Paul. Francesca wanted to laugh. Chantal was jealous of her.

'We are still very close,' Chantal insisted.

'Really, Chantal . . . ' Francesca said impatiently.

The girl's eyes burned with resentment. 'All right, don't believe me. I don't care, but you will see.

'You are such a strange race, you English. If I like a man I show it but you pretend you don't.'

'Do you think I pretended not to like Paul?' Her voice was dull but her eyes were bright with a challenge.

'I am not talking about Paul now. I like Mr. Peter Devlin. He is unlike the young boys who live around here. Outside he is the cool English gentleman but beneath all the ice is the fire. I think I will like breaking the ice.'

Ninon came streaking across the cobbles towards them. She mewed and jumped over the car door into Francesca's lap. The cat looked up at her, mewing plaintively and automatically Francesca stroked her gently.

Hips swinging, humming a little tune, Chantal went off towards the château, leaving Francesca wishing she had the courage to strangle that infuriating child.

5

'It is nice to see you, *chérie.*'

Marguerite Varonne held out her arms to Francesca who placed a kiss on her cheek. Marguerite held her away, studying her daughter-in-law carefully. 'You look much better already, child. I knew all you needed was to be with us, and I was right, wasn't I? I'm sure you've even put on weight just in the few days since you arrived.'

She smiled complacently. Francesca drew away and sank into a high-backed chair. This morning Marguerite Varonne was up and dressed for the first time since Francesca's arrival. They were in the first floor *salon*, a large room which served as a sitting-room for the family. The high windows gave out onto the valley and the sun streamed in, bathing the only two occupants of the room in warmth, which even the coldness of the château could not disperse.

Francesca had steeled herself for this interview. She knew she just could not avoid her mother-in-law indefinitely.

More than a week had passed since her arrival and it had been days since her trip into the village. She hadn't gone in again. She tried to pretend to herself that she wasn't avoiding Peter Devlin, for she could find no good reason why she should do so. But she also told herself that he could not stay indefinitely, and eventually, soon, he would be gone. Until then she would try and restrain her restlessness and remain within the château.

Chantal was rarely home. Francesca had no wish to see her, yet perversely resented her being out, for the only reason could be a man. Peter.

Francesca glanced around her briefly. Obviously all the best furniture that remained had been brought to this room. Without the least pretension of grandeur it was by far the most comfortable and pleasant room Francesca had so far seen.

Marguerite seemed quite happy; so unnaturally happy that for a few moments Francesca was puzzled by it. When Marguerite smiled at her again, Francesca realised at last that Marguerite was still heavily drugged. Her heart gave a lurch of dismay before she came to the conclusion that it was probably very necessary.

Her mind went back to her wedding day. Then she had been a frightened eighteen, and the presence of Paul's mother terrified her. The terror had remained with her although she saw little of Marguerite during her marriage. Now it seemed so foolish to have feared this pathetic woman who had no future, only a past. All Francesca felt now was pity.

But, even possessing the fogged mind of the chronic sick, Marguerite still retained her exquisite sense of dress. It was something she had passed on to her son; Paul always looked immaculate. His taste was also peerless, so much so that Francesca never demurred when he insisted on choosing her clothes too.

His choice was always the right one. The clothes she wore now were all expensive, all chosen by him. Since his death she hadn't bought one garment.

Today Marguerite was wearing a simple dress of fine wool, its only decoration being a diamond brooch — a phoenix rising from the ashes, the whole motif enclosed in a large V.

'Yes, you do look much better,' Marguerite said again. 'You realise we have been very worried about you.'

'There was no need, Maman. I was in good hands.'

'Of course. For a Varonne there can be nothing but the best. But Paul was so miserable without you all these months. He's so glad to have you with him, and that is how it should be even though I've seen so little of you since you came. I understand though. You and Paul have seen little of each other for months now, it is only natural you will want only his company just now — and he will want to see you of course. Don't think I resent seeing less of him now, because

116

I don't — truly.' She sighed and started blankly into space. 'I don't see him at all now.'

Francesca swallowed. She tried to speak but no words would come.

'I was not happy when you were married. I expect you knew that, but I know now I was wrong. You are the right wife for my son.'

Francesca felt sick. She knew she just couldn't bear much more of this however hard she tried. Talking of Paul's death could not be so painful.

Marguerite smiled. 'Berthe tells me Chantal is seeing a great deal of an Englishman who is staying in the village.' She gave a little laugh and Francesca's heart fluttered unevenly. 'However hard we try to remain totally French in this family we cannot escape connections with England.'

The door opened and Jeanne came in bearing a heavy silver tray. She placed it on the table near to Francesca.

Marguerite beamed at the girl. '*Merci*, Jeanne.'

After the girl had gone Marguerite fluttered one beringed hand towards the tray. 'Do pour, *chérie*. That pot is an old family heirloom and far too heavy for my poor wrists.'

Despite her frailty of looks and her mental weakness Francesca was convinced that her mother-in-law possessed quite considerable strength. However, she was glad of something to do. The coffee pot was indeed heavy. It was solid silver, chased into an intricate pattern, and scored from constant use. The cups were Sèvres, and so dainty that Francesca was afraid of touching them. In Marguerite's hand they were well-placed; Francesca felt her fingers might crush the delicate china.

She gazed across the room at the dusty portrait in a gilt frame. The portrait fascinated Francesca. The man proudly gazing back at her from the canvas, despite wearing the ornate clothes of his period, was clearly a Varonne. He possessed a remarkable likeness to both Julien and Paul.

Marguerite glanced round at the portrait and back at Francesca. Her smile was one of amusement. 'You cannot help but be interested in our history, Francesca. To be a Varonne is to be part of history, even though you have never considered it important to have roots firmly in the past.'

Francesca looked startled. 'That's not so, Maman. Of course it's interesting, but my family were very ordinary. Naturally, now I'm here, I am interested, and if Paul had brought me before . . . ' she quickly stopped herself saying 'before his death,' and went on quickly, 'before now I would have been far more interested than I have been.'

'You will learn,' she said, nodding her head, 'and you will come to be proud of bearing our name. That portrait is an old one, but unfortunately it is not a valuable one — except to us.'

'Who is he?'

'Henri de Varonne. He lived here in 1441 or thereabouts when there was a fortified castle on this very spot. The

Varonnes relinquished the 'de' during the revolution. Henri, it is said, abducted a young girl and raped her. She jumped from the battlements when he finally released her.'

'Is that the gypsy girl who put a curse on the family before she died?' Francesca asked.

It was Marguerite's turn to look startled, and then, disbelieving. 'There is some such rumour which still persists. I doubt if there is any truth in it.' She pointed to another portrait; a small one of a woman in Elizabethan dress. 'That lady is Emiline de Varonne. She poisoned the man she was to marry so that she could marry his younger brother. It is suspected that she poisoned several other people who got in the way of her ambitions.'

Francesca gave a broken little laugh. 'You must be proud of the family you married into.'

'It would be pointless to be ashamed. All these events are now in the realms of history.'

Marguerite stirred her coffee thoughtfully, added an extra measure of cream, and said, 'Yes, it is to be hoped that Chantal will soon settle down. I know it would relieve Berthe and Julien of much of their anxiety. All she needs is a husband and a few children.' She took a wafer-thin biscuit from the plate. Francesca hadn't yet started her coffee. 'You too, Francesca,' she added, glancing over her cup and wagging one tiny finger.

'Me?' echoed Francesca.

'Yes, of course. Do not look so surprised. Surely it has occurred to you. You have been married — it must be five years now. It is time you and Paul began to consider children again.'

'Again,' Francesca repeated stupidly.

Marguerite put down the cup carefully. 'You don't mind my talking plainly to you?'

Francesca shook her head. 'Not at all,' she managed to say in a remarkably firm voice. She must remember that Marguerite was ill, her mind was not clear.

'I am glad. You have no mother and I have only one child. I would like us to be close. I think we can be now you have come to live here. I never liked the life you and Paul lived in London.'

'But I haven't . . . ' Francesca broke off. It was useless to argue. If that was what Marguerite believed, it would be cruel to try and even reason with her. 'What did you mean by considering children *again*, Maman?'

'Now, *chérie*, there is nothing to be gained by pretending it didn't happen. It is very unfortunate when a woman loses a baby but not the end of the world, although she can be forgiven for thinking so at the time.'

Francesca's eyes grew round and her cup clattered into the saucer. It sounded like the tinkle of a tiny bell.

'It was a pity you were so ill afterwards, but now you are here I don't think it will be long before you are bringing me good news. I know Paul is anxious to continue the family name. It is imperative, and he has been very negligent in that direction so far.'

Francesca's hands were trembling. She attempted to put the cup and saucer down but her eyes were blurred with tears and the china knocked against the side of the table and went crashing to the floor.

She jumped to her feet as Marguerite gave out a little cry. 'I'm sorry,' Francesca gasped. She picked up her bag and rushed towards the door, saying over her shoulder, 'I'll get someone to sweep it up.'

She choked back a sob. As she closed the door thankfully behind her Marguerite was on her knees picking up each precious piece.

Francesca sank back against the wall. What had given her such a grotesque idea? She turned her face to the cold stone wall, willing back the tears. I can't bear it any longer, she told herself. Not one moment longer.

She straightened up. She must tell Berthe. Explain that the meanderings of Marguerite's mind were too distressing for her to bear any more. Berthe must make an excuse for her absence for the rest of the stay. Berthe could explain that she was with Paul, seeing the country-side together.

A strangled laugh came from deep in her throat. I shall soon start to believe it too, she thought. I'll soon be as mad as Marguerite.

She brushed her hair back from her damp cheeks and smoothed the skirt of her dress. As she did so a cool breeze ruffled it against her knees and she looked sharply towards the end of the corridor from which it came, hoping that Berthe would not come to fuss over her in her usual fashion. She wanted to see no one just now.

The door at the end of the corridor had opened. It led to one of the disused wings of the château. Ninon streaked past, brushing close to Francesca's legs as she passed. The feel of the animal's fur against her bare legs made her shudder convulsively.

She stared into the gloom, and then

it was as if her very blood was frozen in her veins. For a moment she couldn't move, or utter a cry, and then she began to run. Someone called her name. The unmistakable perfume of *Hombre* pursued her down the corridor. Someone called out to her again, but her legs could not carry her away fast enough. She came to the central landing and paused, breathlessly, wondering which way to turn. She wasn't aware of having made any noise, but she realised she had screamed and her shoes were clattering loudly on the stone floor.

She fled down the stairs, aware of Berthe's upturned face below. Suddenly, stumbling down the last two steps Francesca found herself being clasped tightly in Berthe's strong arms.

'*Mon dieu!* You must not run down the stairs in such a way. Some of the stones are worn. You could have broken your neck. What is it, child? You look as if *le diable* himself was after you.'

'It was Paul I saw,' she gasped. 'I saw Paul!'

Berthe held her away, searching her face anxiously. '*Paul*,' she said in a whisper. 'What nonsense is this? You are imagining this. How can you have seen *Paul*?' Her hands tightened on Francesca's shoulders. 'You are still overwrought, Francesca, but don't let yourself give way like this. It is impossible, and you know it.'

'I tell you I saw him! Do you think I wouldn't know him? My own husband?'

'I think you are still very much upset and Marguerite has upset you further. What has she been saying to you this time? Tell me Francesca.'

Francesca winced under Berthe's grip. At the sound of footsteps coming down the stairs she tore herself from Berthe's arms and turned round. Julien came hurrying down towards them and his face was creased with concern.

'Francesca, *ma chérie*, why did you run when I called to you?'

Francesca stared at him in disbelief and he looked at Berthe in dismay. 'Is she all right?'

Berthe nodded. 'Was it you she saw,

Julien? That explains it.'

'I have been in the west wing, checking on its state of repair. It is already three months since I last went, and when I came out Francesca was just coming from the *salon*, and she bolted down the corridor. I called to her but she did not stop.'

'She thought you were Paul. She'd been with Marguerite. You know how distressing that can be.'

Julien murmured his agreement and put his hand on Francesca's shoulder. 'I am sorry I frightened you, *chérie*.'

Francesca took a deep breath. 'It's all right, Julien. I don't know how I could have been so foolish. But it's true, Maman was rambling and I just can't get used to it.' She took another deep breath. 'I haven't had as long as you to accustom myself to listening to her. I'm sorry I startled you both.'

'It is dark in the corridors,' Berthe explained. 'Look Francesca, Julien is very much like Paul superficially. His height, his weight. There was always a considerable likeness. It was often remarked upon.'

Francesca nodded wearily. 'I'm a fool. I don't really know what possessed me to panic.'

'No, no, *chérie*, do not apologise any more. It is understandable. You have been very ill and I'm quite sure you cannot be entirely recovered. That is why you act strangely at times.'

'I'm not mad!'

She backed away from them both. 'No, of course you're not mad,' Berthe said soothingly, 'only you must understand why sometimes things upset you more than they would upset us.'

Francesca's eyes narrowed fractionally when she looked at Julien. His face revealed nothing but concern for her. 'How long have you worn Paul's after shave lotion?'

His hand went automatically to his smooth cheek. 'Since Paul bought me a bottle last Christmas. I don't really like it. I don't use it often; only when my own astringent runs out, as it did today.'

She shrank away from him even further, almost back into Berthe's arms. 'Come,' she said, 'you must rest. You have had a nasty shock. I think, Julien, we must seriously consider putting more lights in the corridors. We cannot have a recurrence of what has happened today.'

'I agree, *chérie*. It will be done as soon as I can make the arrangements with the electrician.'

Berthe began to lead Francesca towards the step, but she broke away. 'If you don't mind, I'd rather get some fresh air.'

She was still badly shaken, more from alarm at having made such an obvious mistake.

Berthe started after her. 'Would you like me to come with you? You surely cannot go alone.'

Francesca shuddered yet again. They were becoming as solicitous of her as they were of poor Marguerite.

'I think I prefer my own company just now,' she answered quietly.

She walked slowly to the door and opened it, aware that Berthe and Julien were watching her all the time. She walked out into the beckoning sunshine. It was like the parting of the waters to a drowning man. She walked very slowly until she had passed through the gateway and then she began to run as fast as she could.

By the time she came to the bottom of the hill she was breathless, but if she'd been forced to crawl all the way she would have come away from that place. It was slowly destroying her.

Her thoughts were totally dispirited as she walked, slowly now, down steep streets flanked by grey houses. She knew that however long she stayed out, eventually she must go back. At the very thought of it she was filled with revulsion, and the fear that she might, indeed, be bordering on insanity.

She was so filled with fearful thoughts that she hardly noticed where she was walking, and as he came out of the post office, she cannoned into the last person she wanted to see just then — Peter.

For a moment he held her against him to steady her. His freshly shaved cheek smelled faintly of lime. It was like a breath of fresh air.

She was still out of breath from her mad dash down the hill and she gasped as he caught her. He took off his sunglasses and held her away from him.

'Oh, it's you,' she said in an effort to appear nonchalant, aware that she was failing miserably. Just the sight of him always managed to put her morbid little fears into their right proportion.

She didn't like the château, which was reasonable as she had always lived in much cosier places. She didn't like its atmosphere or its history — much of it bloody — and she felt that many of the long-dead Varonnes could have been cruel. But her dislike of the château was no reason to let her imagination take hold of her again. This time reason might not return so easily.

'Yes, I'm afraid it is,' he answered,

smiling wryly. He scrutinised her face and his smile faded. 'You look ghastly, absolutely ghastly; did you know that? What are they doing to you up there? Keeping you a prisoner in one of the tower rooms?'

She laughed with a forced gaiety. 'Nothing like that. It's a spooky old place and the atmosphere gets a bit too much for me at times; that's all.'

'Mm,' he murmured, still looking at her curiously.

He sounded disbelieving but she couldn't explain any more. How could she tell him she had amost driven herself to the point of hysteria just because Julien had a faint resemblance to Paul? As if it could have been anyone but Julien. If she told Peter what had happened to her this morning he would only shrink away from her. It had happened to her before, and she had suffered the frustration of disbelief and isolation. Now she could understand it — she, herself, had shrunk away from Marguerite's imaginings. But Francesca was not going to allow it to happen to her again.

To escape his scrutiny she looked past him, into the post office, half-expecting Chantal to follow him out.

'You do need cheering up,' he told her, and that was a statement she couldn't dispute. 'You're lucky I'm just the man to do it. You're having lunch with me today.'

She began to protest. Becoming involved with him, with any man, could only add to her emotional problems.

He did not relinquish his grip on her arm. 'No, Francesca, I am not listening to any arguments today. Your relatives can manage without you for the next few hours.' She recognised that his tone brooked no argument.

She relaxed a little then and no longer had to be led like an unwilling child; she went willingly. Why not? She knew that of anything she wanted his company most of all.

His car was parked nearby, in one of the narrow little streets that ran into the square. He handed her into it and she sank into the seat, wishing she need never go back to the château. When she was with this man it all seemed unreal, yet she was still a Varonne and the family feeling was strong; she could not escape so easily.

She glanced at him. She neither knew nor cared where they were going. Sufficient that it was with him, and away from the château.

When she first met him at Bordeaux she gained an impression of a cold man, but since then he had discarded the formality of a suit and the two occasions on which they had met since her arrival he had worn casual sweaters and slacks. With his suit he had also discarded his coldness — if, indeed, it had been that. It could have been the infamous British reserve. Remembering her reluctance to go with him each time they met, it was possible he could accuse her of that too.

Unlike Chantal. The thought of the girl caused her heart to lurch painfully.

No one could be less reserved than Chantal. How much was she the cause of his good humour? Francesca wondered.

'So, you still find St. Marcel interesting, even after being here more than a week?' she asked after a while, unable to help herself. Curiosity finally got the better of reserve.

'I could stay for a month and still find it interesting.'

His tone, she thought, was cleverly non-committal. He glanced across at her. She was aware that her tension was dispersing like early morning mist in the sun.

'I've been getting around since I saw you last. Yesterday I was at Les Eyzies. Have you been yet?'

She settled into the corner so that she was facing him. 'No, but I believe it's very interesting.'

He laughed. 'Chantal thought so. Believe it or not she's lived here for eighteen years and it was the first time she'd visited the caves.'

She did believe it. The last thing that would interest Chantal was ancient monuments. Peter was the attraction — surely he knew it — not the cave paintings. She felt a sickness deep down inside her at the thought of him spending the day with Chantal.

Chantal yesterday, me today. 'You certainly like to spread your favours around,' she retorted, and hated herself for saying it.

'I enjoy good company,' he answered blandly, and momentarily she hated him too.

The road followed the course of the river. They passed the woods and the cornfields that she had only so far seen from the heights of the château windows. Soon the narrow tributary joined the Dordogne and they followed a wider road lined with poplars that threw elongated shadows across the road.

'What have you been doing apart from educating Chantal?' she asked after a while, anxious to atone for her own waspishness. He was a man on holiday alone; he had a right to choose any one he wished to bear him company. She knew that she had nothing to complain of in his treatment of her. 'Have you done any more fishing?'

He laughed again. 'No! That's one pastime I've given up for the moment. I've just been loafing around. I'm afraid I can't admit to doing anything remarkable since we last met. I've visited one or two of the local châteaux. Most of all I'm enjoying the cooking the area's best known for. Perigord is called the birthplace of good cooking. I suppose you've noticed.'

'I never imagined you to be a gourmet.'

'I'm not. Far from it, but when one lives alone eating tends to become very much a secondary preoccupation, and sometimes non-existent.'

She gave a harsh laugh. 'Don't I know it.'

Their destination turned out to be a

fairly new hotel on one bank of the river. Despite its proximity to water the hotel had its own swimming pool and it was alive with the multi-colour forms of countless swimming costumes and bikinis.

Francesca smiled with pleasure at the sight of so much genuine enjoyment. It seemed so long since she had felt spontaneous joy.

'Fancy a swim before lunch?' he asked when he saw her envious look in the direction of the pool.

'I'd love it, but I have no costume with me.'

'That's easily remedied. There's a shop inside that sells them.' He started towards the main entrance to the hotel before she could protest. 'You wait there, Francesca and I'll be back in two minutes. If you go you'll be there all day just deciding which colour to buy.'

She laughed. 'You are a fool! You don't even know what size I take.'

'Yes I do. Junior miss by the look of you.'

Before she could protest further he was gone. She waited a few minutes, watching rather enviously a French family of parents and two young children having fun in the water, and then she went to find him.

He was coming out the hotel already, the package in his hand neatly wrapped. 'Off you go to the cabins and I'll meet you at the pool.' He gave her the costume and a gaily striped towel. 'You leave the towel in the cabin when you've finished. It's all part of the service.'

'What about you?'

'I've got mine on already. I've taken a swim every day since I came. I make it a habit so I was prepared.'

He was already at the pool when she came out of the cabin. He was sitting at the shallow end, toes in the water, issuing some helpful instructions to two German girls who were laughing up at him. Her first impression of an athletic frame was proved right, and his white swimming trunks showed off splendidly his newly acquired tan.

He caught sight of her when she was halfway across the tiles surrounding the pool and he let out a long, low wolf whistle. The swimsuit did, to her amazement, fit perfectly. It was black, which suited her colouring, and far more simply and modestly styled than any other she possessed. Paul's taste rarely lent itself to the simple or the modest.

'Are you complimenting me, or your own taste?' she asked lightly.

'What do you think?' he asked, casting a deliberately lascivious smile over her body.

'I think you've had practice at buying women's clothes before.'

He looked down at the impossibly blue water of the pool. 'A little. A little, Francesca.'

He jumped to his feet easily, tapped her playfully on the behind and said briskly, 'Come on, I'll race you to the other end.'

He was, of course, an easy winner.

From that moment, it seemed she hardly stopped laughing, and the sound of her own laughter in her ears was still strange.

After their swim they changed and had drinks by the pool. Her hair soon dried and began to fluff out in the sun, his, being thicker, remained damply plastered around his head.

'You were speaking German to those girls, weren't you?' she asked as she sipped at an ice-cold Campari.

'Yes, that's right. Do you speak any German?'

She shook her head. 'Being married for five years to a man who was, to all intents and purposes, French, I don't even speak that language. How many do you speak?'

He drained the last of his whisky from the glass and put it down. The pool was almost empty of people now, the promise of food being the more alluring. 'If I tell you you'd accuse me of bragging.'

'I promise I won't.'

'I can speak French, German and Italian fluently, and Spanish fairly well.

I can get by with Scandinavian and Russian when pressed.'

'Wow! Don't say any more. You make me feel ashamed.'

'Nonsense. We're all good at something. I was hopeless at maths. My father hoped I'd become a scientist of some sort, but I was consistently bottom of the class in the necessary subjects.'

'You have no need to be ashamed. I really was good at nothing.' He looked at her doubtfully. 'It's true,' she assured him.

'I doubt it. We all have something we're good at. For a woman it's often sufficient to be a good homemaker or,' he added when she looked away, 'just being good to look at. Making a man happy is an important quality — underrated these days, I think.'

Was he thinking of Chantal? she wondered.

'Think what a dull old world it would be if we all had the brains and looks of Einstein.'

She smiled at him then and he asked,

'What did you do before you were married?'

'Not very much. I took a shorthand and typing course and got a job with a firm that manufactured machine parts. That's how I met Paul. He was working for them too at the time. When we got married I gave up work. He didn't believe in wives working. I suppose if I'd had a career of any importance it would have been different.'

'He must have been the sort of man who prefers his wife at his beck and call.'

She gave a little laugh. 'Something like that.'

'Will you go back to work when you go back to England?'

'I'll have to take a refresher course, I suppose, but I definitely want a job. Something interesting and absorbing if possible. I'm going to get a smaller flat when I go home, so there'll be little enough to occupy me there, and I don't like to be idle. A job is essential from that point of view.'

'For the money?'

'No,' she answered. 'Paul left me well-provided for. When he died I was too shocked to even care about that part of it, but a week or two later I had a visit from a solicitor. He'd seen the news reports of Paul's death and was expecting a call from me. It seems that he had drawn up Paul's will some time before his death and wondered if I knew anything about it.

'I didn't, of course. The solicitor had the will and I found a copy, sure enough, in a drawer in his desk according to the instructions he had left with the solicitor. Up until then I had no idea we were so well-off, even though we lived well and there was never any shortage of money. I never had anything to do with money. Paul attended to everything in that department. He had a good job, I knew that of course. The only thing that really surprised me was the fact that he'd made a will at all. It wasn't at all like Paul to do a thing like that. He was the type of man who never thought about the serious things in life.'

'Lucky for you that he did. It's always best for a man who travels a great deal to attend to such matters.'

'Yes, well, as it turned out it was providential that he did. Everything was so much simpler, otherwise I wouldn't have known what to do.'

'Surely there were friends and relatives who came to your aid?'

'I have no relatives of my own now, and the Varonnes were all here and had enough to cope with. As for friends,' she gave a little smile, 'there was no one I could think of to lean on. My father always said that whatever misfortunes come our way, whatever mistakes we make, they're never in vain, provided that we learn from them. Since Paul died I've learned to stand on my own two feet for the first time in my life. I'll never be afraid of being alone again.'

His eyes held hers for a moment longer and then, deliberately, he looked at his watch. 'I think it's time we took our table.'

6

Lunch was served on a terrace over-looking the pool. The gay splashings were, for the moment, stilled. Only the gentle breeze ruffled its surface.

The menu that had been presented to Francesca was enormous. One glance at it and she gave up. 'You'd better order for both of us, Peter, otherwise it might take me until dinner time to decipher all this.'

She waited until the *maitre d'* had retired with their order and then asked what they were going to have.

'We begin with trout, which I'm assured comes from the river yonder,' he indicated the strip of water with a jerk of his head. 'Then we're having onion soup — it's amazing how you can never get anything like it outside France. And the head waiter tells me there is nothing to equal the chef's tournados — *avec truffes*, of course.'

'Of course,' she agreed with mock solemnity, 'we mustn't miss out the truffles.'

He put down the wine menu and looked at her. 'And it's all to be helped down by a bottle of good Chablis. I told the waiter we'll decide on the sweet later.'

She laughed. 'Seriously, Peter, I'll never manage all that. I couldn't.'

'Nonsense. You can and you will. Heaven knows you could do with some extra flesh on your bones. I'm going to eat everything and so will you, even if it's to stop me looking like a glutton. For me this is quite a change from burnt bangers and rubbery eggs.'

She laughed again, although the underlying truth of his words filled her with a strange sort of melancholy. For all women being the weaker sex, there was nothing more pathetic than a man coping on his own.

To her own surprise Francesca found she was hungry. The combination of fresh air, the swim, and her total lack of tension gave her back her lost appetite.

'Do you realise the importance these little truffles play in the fame of Perigord gastronomy?' he asked as his knife cut into his steak as if it were butter. 'And they're better, at half the price, than they would be in Paris or London.'

'That's not so surprising when they come from this very area.' She gave a little laugh. 'Do you know, until I married Paul I believed truffles were just chocolates?'

He grinned at her. 'So did I.' He jerked his hand in the direction of the river again. 'See those trees on the other bank? They're the truffle-oaks.'

'Really? Which part of the tree do they grow on?'

'The roots.' He swallowed the last piece of steak. 'They're virtually unde-tectable so dogs are used to smell them out, and then they're dug up from the roots.'

Francesca wrinkled her nose. 'I'm

glad you've told me *after* I've finished. Who would ever believe something that looks so revolting could be so delicious?'

His head was back in the menu. He glanced up at her. 'What are you having next?'

Her eyes grew large. 'Peter, I can't manage anything else.'

'Yes, you can. You've eaten everything so far, despite what you said when we ordered. Try some of their strawberry mousse. You won't be sorry, I promise you.'

She looked at him, wondering where his knowledge of the menu came from. It occurred to her that he had already been here with Chantal, but she was determined not to let such speculation spoil her enjoyment of his company today. It was enough that she was with him now.

She grinned. 'All right. I will try it.'

He gave the order to the waiter and turned to refill her wineglass. Too late, she covered it with her hand. 'No, I really shouldn't have any more. I've had far too much already. I'm beginning to feel lightheaded.'

'Come on, don't be faint hearted,' he chided. 'This stuff puts good red blood into your veins.'

'Then perhaps I had better drink it,' she said dryly.

It wasn't until coffee was brought that she spoke again. 'I don't know when I've eaten so much at one time,' she said, handing him his cup.

He eyed her thoughtfully for a moment. 'What exactly ailed you this morning, Francesca?' he asked, stirring his coffee slowly.

He had chosen a good time to ask. Their lighthearted conversation, the good food and wine, had made her carefree. She wondered if he had purposely chosen his time to ask. What had troubled her this morning was no longer of any importance. How foolish it all seemed now. Marguerite's harmless meandering mind could only hurt her if she let it.

Nevertheless, she gave a little sigh and carefully refolded her linen napkin along its original creases. 'I told you that my mother-in-law was ill . . . ' She glanced at him briefly and he was still watching her. 'Well, it's mental. She refused to accept that Paul is dead and she talks about him as if he were still alive.'

'I can understand how distressing that can be,' he murmured.

'The worst part is that I found out this morning she's also got it into her head, for some reason, that I had a miscarriage and that's why I was ill.'

'And had you?'

She toyed with the lid of the coffee pot. 'No.'

'It's a pity you didn't have children, Francesca. It would have helped you. You wouldn't have been so alone.'

'You mean, I'd have had someone else to consider apart from myself?'

'Yes.'

'You're right, I suppose. I did become rather wrapped up in myself. If I'd had a child I would have had to consider it instead and I would have had someone to look after. It's too late to think about that now. One doesn't think of being left alone at twenty-three.'

'Did you never want children?'

'I never gave it much thought, Peter, and if Paul did he never said so. There was always so much time . . . '

'Is your mother-in-law being difficult with you, apart from what you've just told me. You said, the day I brought you from the airport, that you and she didn't get on very well.'

'It was only my impression. I was never very sure of myself. I don't think she resents me any more. There aren't many Varonnes left now, and the family feeling is strong. I think my being a Varonne overcomes any personal animosity she might feel towards me. Besides, she thinks it's time we had a family . . . '

'It's odd the way sick minds work,' he murmured and she answered, 'Yes,' in a very small voice.

A moment later she said, 'When I left you the other day Chantal told me that Paul's body was never recovered from the river. It shook me. There's something even more horrible than death when a body is never found.'

He looked at her briefly. 'I had heard but I didn't consider myself the one to tell you. I don't think Chantal was either.'

'You know a lot about what goes on in St. Marcel, Peter.'

'Madame Oisin talks a lot and there aren't many guests in the hotel for her to talk to.' Then he asked briskly. 'Shall we go and sit by the river for a while?'

She smiled and nodded, glad of the break. The turf that sloped down to the water's edge might have been cut from a piece of green velvet. Peter put his arm loosely around her waist and led the way to an ancient chestnut tree which was almost at the river's edge. Its luxuriant branches gave welcome shade from the afternoon sun.

Francesca walked right to the water's

edge and peered into the river. The sparkling water was translucent in the sunlight, reflecting her face clearly on its surface.

'I can actually see the fish in here!' she cried a moment later. 'Come and see, Peter.'

'Oh, I have seen them,' he answered lazily. 'The trouble is they always see me too.'

He had settled down against the tree trunk and waved her over. When she reached his side he took her hand and drew her down beside him, bringing out the silver cigarette case.

He flicked it open. The engraving, *Love is for ever, K* sparkled in the sunlight filtering through the branches overhead. Francesca drew her eyes away and shook her head. She looked at the gently moving water, listening to its placid gurgle as it flowed to the sea.

At her side Peter took out a cigarette and closed the case with a snap. When she looked at him again he was smoking the cigarette and gazing across to the far side of the river.

For a man like Peter Devlin there was always a woman in his life. A woman whose name began with K. He would go back to her after his holiday, taking with him only a few pleasant memories of a girl he had pitied; and even those memories would soon fade.

Her own memories would fade less quickly, for she was aware that feelings for him were stirring inside her. It would be useless to deny them to herself any longer.

So soon. Could it be? she asked herself.

He leaned back against the tree trunk. 'Why didn't you come sooner, Francesca?' he asked thoughtfully, blowing smoke rings into the air.

'My doctor wouldn't let me come when it happened — I was too shocked — and later I was really ill for a couple of months.' He looked at her and she gave him a hesitant glance. 'I had what is commonly called a nervous breakdown.'

'You don't have to feel guilty about that. You had one of the gravest shocks you'll ever have to suffer, with no chance to prepare yourself for it.'

'I know, but the knowledge doesn't help because I was fully aware of what was happening to me and I was powerless to prevent it.'

'Few of us are.' She looked at him curiously. 'You must have had someone to fall back on, Francesca. You can't seriously mean that you were entirely alone in the world. Or were you just too proud to ask for help?'

'There isn't anyone. My parents were elderly. We lived with my mother's spinster sister and she looked after me when they died, one after the other. My aunt died just after I met Paul. That's why we didn't wait long to get married.

'And friends. There were dozens. At least I thought there were. We were hardly ever at home, and when we were it was to entertain hordes of people. Paul was a very great socialite. He got on very well with everyone and had acquaintances by the score. It wasn't until he died that I discovered they weren't our friends at all, they were his.

'A few of the closest ones rallied round me when he was killed. He was always so full of life it was hard for anyone to believe he'd never be the life and soul of a party again.' She looked down at the turf and pulling an overlong blade she twisted it round her finger. 'They did try to be kind but I soon started to embarrass them with things I began to imagine, and before very long they left me alone.'

'What did you imagine?'

'When Paul died I was shocked; grief-stricken I suppose. That everyone took as normal, but it was a couple of months later that the real trouble started, although it was all to do with the shock of his death.'

'Trouble?' he asked, frowning slightly.

Suddenly she knew she would have to talk about it, and that Peter Devlin would not turn away from her in disgust.

'I began to imagine that the flat was being watched. When I went out I was convinced I was being followed. The man who stood next to me at the bus stop was suspect, the woman behind me in the queue at the greengrocer. It was horrible, but I couldn't stop myself suspecting everyone. No one would believe me. I knew I was being a fool but I really believed I was being watched and followed, even though I kept telling myself it was only my imagination.

'There was a flat next to ours. It had been empty for months and then a married couple moved in just before Paul died. I even suspected them. The woman tried to become friendly but I just slammed the door in her face.

'I had an obsession that our flat had been searched and my things had been moved out of place. As if one could tell!

'Matters became so bad that I'd cower for days in the flat and sit in the dark all night without bothering to eat or go to bed, afraid to go out because someone was watching. And when I did go out I'd walk for hours rather than go back.

'Eventually I knew I had to have help. The doctor was sympathetic. He recommended a psychiatrist and I went into a nursing home that specialised in mental cases.' She smiled at him apologetically but he looked away. 'I knew it was my only salvation. And it was. I'm fine now. No more imagining, thank goodness.'

'Didn't you think of going to the police if you believed all this was happening to you?' he asked without looking at her.

'It was the first thing I did, but that was at the beginning, before I began to question my own sanity. They sent someone round to interview me, promised to keep an eye on the flat. Presumably they did. They couldn't arrest the gremlins that were in my own mind. I ended up by accusing the sergeant at the police station of being in league with a conspiracy! That finished it for me. They get nuts like that in every day.'

'Don't say that,' he snapped.

'I shouldn't. It's no joke. The mind is a very delicate thing. When I look at poor Maman I realise how lucky I am.'

'Don't, Francesca,' he said. 'You are nothing like her. There can be no comparison.'

She smiled, feeling a rush of warmth at his concern. 'And there's no need for you to feel bad on my behalf,' she said softly. 'I don't want pity any more. Once I did; I enjoyed wallowing in pity, but I gave up feeling sorry for myself a long time ago.'

'You've been through a very bad experience and pity isn't something you should despise.'

'You've been kind enough to listen. I appreciate that. It's good to talk, Peter. People say they understand, but they don't — not really. They couldn't. But I feel that you really do.'

He put his hand over hers. 'Yes, I do, Francesca.' He looked down at the hand that covered hers. 'I can easily understand the way you were knocked off balance. Something like it happened to me, three years ago when my wife died.'

She looked away in confusion. 'I've had so much said to me since Paul died, you'd think I could find the right words to say to you now.'

'I don't want you to say anything. I've only mentioned it because I want you to know it does get better. It may be hard for you to believe that right now. The pain is always there, but the edge is dulled.'

He withdrew his hand and pulled out his cigarette case again. This time she accepted one. After he had lit it she asked, 'What was her name?'

'Kaye. The case was her wedding present to me. The words are ironic, aren't they?'

'Was it an accident too?'

He shook his head. 'No, but I was no more prepared than you. She started having headaches. At first it wasn't much; it became something of a joke between us when she used to say she had one of her 'heads'. The family doctor thought she was neurotic. After a while he even prescribed another child — we already had a daughter. She wasn't neurotic though. She wasn't the type even to complain. When the headaches got worse the doctor wanted her to go to the hospital, but she kept putting it off as healthy people often do.

'One evening I came home and found her terribly ill. I bundled her, and the baby, in the car and drove to the hospital as quickly as I could. By the time we got there she was unconscious. She died two days later without coming round at all.'

Francesca was appalled. For months she had been so wrapped up in herself she had forgotten that other people suffered too. 'What on earth was wrong?'

'A brain tumour. It didn't show up on the X-rays; they even showed me the plates. It was no one's fault that she died. It would have happened anyway. Even if she'd gone earlier there wasn't a thing they could have done for her.'

'But you didn't crack up. People do suffer loss and they don't go all to pieces like I did. I knew it all the time, yet I couldn't help myself. That's what appals me about myself most of all; I let myself get into the state where I was heading towards insanity. I can't understand why I didn't take a hold of myself while I had the chance.'

'Not everyone follows the same pattern of behaviour. My own little insanity was in blaming the doctor. I spent hours just walking around planning revenge on him. But it passes.'

'Yes, I know.'

He got to his feet and held out his hand to her. 'It's time we were moving.'

For a moment she stayed there, unwilling to move. She had the impulse to say, 'I don't want to go back — ever,' but she fought it back.

Taking one last look round, storing the memory for a time when she was lonely again, she gave him her hand and he hauled her to her feet.

'What is your daughter's name?' she asked as she brushed the grass from her skirt.

'Diana.'

She glanced up at him. How she envied him his tranquillity, his ability to come to terms with his loss. Francesca hoped she would one day find such peace of mind, but never while she remained at the château.

'How old is she now?'

He smiled. 'Five and a half, and growing fast.' They started back towards the hotel. 'Will you help me do something, Francesca?'

'If I can. What is it you want?'

He smiled again. 'Come into the hotel and I'll show you.'

Mystified she followed him through the lobby to a small arcade of shops. Next to the shop where he had brought her swimsuit there was a souvenir kiosk.

The saleslady beamed in anticipation when Peter picked up one of the dolls set out on the counter. 'I want to take one back for Diana, but I've no idea which one. Which would you suggest?'

Francesca gazed at the dazzling array of gifts with their equally dazzling price tags. 'You really want me to choose?'

'I'd always understood that women knew more about this kind of thing than men,' he answered wryly.

'It's so hard to choose,' she murmured a moment later as she happily examined each one, aware that he was just watching her and making no attempt to help.

He picked one up and turned it over. 'How about this one. She's wearing very sexy underwear.'

Francesca laughed and, taking the miniature woman from him, she put it back onto the counter. '*That* certainly isn't suitable for a child. It's more the type of souvenir a lecherous salesman might take home for his equally lecherous friend.'

'I'm glad you haven't put me in that category, but you must remember that you don't know me at all well.'

She smiled back at him. 'I think I do, besides, if my memory serves me well, you're not a salesman.'

'For the rest, you'll just have to wait and find out, won't you?'

She laughed but it was self-consciously. The saleslady suggested another doll with a rigid patience born of long experience. Francesca shook her head and pointed to one she had just noticed on a shelf behind the counter. The woman lifted it down.

'That's the one,' said Francesca, looking at it with delight.

'It's a costume doll.'

'What better gift than a doll wearing the dress of the region? I'm willing to bet she's got several of the ordinary kind. Any little girl would love a doll like this, but if you're not sure . . . '

He grinned and handed the doll over for wrapping. 'I knew you were the best one to choose for me.'

'It's the least I could do,' she answered demurely, 'after you'd bought me that swimsuit and the meal. I only hope Diana gets as much pleasure playing with it as I did from choosing it.'

With the doll safely wrapped and under his arm they went back to the car. Again Francesca experienced a pang of regret. No use pretending any longer that he meant nothing to her; he was beginning to mean a lot.

'Where is Diana now?' she asked as the car sped back along the road to St. Marcel far too quickly.

He grinned, keeping his eyes firmly on the road ahead. 'Women!' he said with mock exasperation. 'Mention a child, and a fellow is forgotten completely.'

'All right, let's talk about you instead.'

'I've talked quite enough about myself already. I'm not at all interesting. Diana lives with my wife's parents. When Kaye died I was in no position to care for a child, and they were. She helped them a lot as you can imagine. I often work abroad so it's a good arrangement, otherwise I would have had to take in a housekeeper. I sold our house and took a flat nearby my in-laws, so I do see her almost every day.'

'Wouldn't you rather spend your holiday with her?'

'Naturally, but she's still at school at the moment. Later, during the school holidays we're going to the seaside together. We're both looking forward to it.'

'You get a lot of holidays.'

'It's one of the perks of the job.'

It was far too soon when the car pulled up on the terrace in front of the château. It was a repetition of her arrival more than a week before. So much had happened since then.

After being away from the château, with him, Francesca was aware more than ever before the shadow of gloom it cast over her.

As if aware of her thoughts he said softly, 'You could always go back home, you know.'

She hadn't yet heard from the estate

agent. It was far too soon for him to have disposed of the lease of the flat. Suddenly she knew she was never going back to it.

'I can't. Not so soon. It's been less than a fortnight. I think they expect me to stay here for good. I'm a Varonne and this is where the Varonnes live. I haven't even the excuse that I have a home and a family to return to.'

'You have a life to return to.'

She gave a hollow little laugh, quite unlike the spontaneous eruption of joy he usually elicited from her. 'To them, I think, my life is that of Paul's widow.'

'It's an outdated trend in dynastic families, and it's totally selfish and unfair. It's a throwback to the times when a man's widow was buried with him along with his other chattels. But this is the twentieth century, thank heavens.' She shuddered and he put a hand on her shoulder. 'Forgive me for that, Francesca. It's just that I remembered how strained you looked this morning and how carefree you were with me, and I assure you I am not flattering myself.'

She looked up at him, amazed at his anger. 'I've given you the wrong impression, Peter. They've been terribly kind to me, but I am determined to go back to England eventually. I couldn't possibly make my home here, but I must stay a little longer — a month perhaps. Believe me, Peter, being with you today has given me a much needed sense of proportion.'

He smiled then. 'I'm glad. We'll do it again.'

She beamed. 'I'd love to. How long are you staying?'

It was a question she had longed to ask.

He traced his finger around the rim of the wheel. 'For a while longer anyway.' He glanced at her sideways. 'And I'll be seeing you tomorrow night.' Invountarily her heart beat faster. 'I've received an invitation for dinner from Berthe Varonne.'

'That's nice,' she said, aware of the

triteness of her words, but she could hardly speak her true thoughts and tell him she wanted to see him again soon but not amongst the Varonnes; not with Chantal.

'I thought so too,' he answered blandly, peering up at the château.

As if in response to a cue Chantal came swaggering round the corner from the tower entrance. Francesca saw her first and was not surprised at the intrusion. She had almost expected it, yet her spirits took a definite downward turn.

Chantal's lips formed into a knowing smile as she peered in through the open window of the car. 'You must have known I was coming out, Peter. Now I shan't have to walk to the village after all.'

'Why don't you take a car?' Francesca asked snappishly.

Chantal looked amused at her tone. 'Because I like my men to drive *me*,' she retorted. 'If I took a car no one would bring me home at night, and I would miss a lot of fun, wouldn't I, Peter?'

'I doubt it, Chantal,' he answered with a laugh.

Chantal gave Francesca a perfunctory glance. 'I am glad to see you have got over your fright, Francesca. Maman told me all about it. It was a very strange thing to happen to you. You must be sicker than we thought.'

Francesca was aware of Peter's sudden frown. 'I'm quite all right now, thank you,' she murmured.

She got out of the car quickly, before any more could be said, and Chantal sidled into the place she had vacated.

'Thanks for everything, Peter,' Francesca said in a subdued voice.

'A pleasure,' he answered, giving her a formal salute.

Francesca stepped back as he put the car into reverse, but she made no move to go in. As he drove away she could see Chantal's face turned to his and heard his laugh ring out. By the time they reached the village Chantal would have told him of her foolish behaviour this morning. He would know she still imagined things and was tormented by them.

As the car disappeared around the bend Francesca felt the familiar knot of frustration form inside her.

7

'You must have quite a number of tales to tell of events that have happened in this château over the years, Madame Varonne,' said Peter, bestowing a charming smile on his hostess.

Berthe Varonne handed him his coffee. 'Too many to relate this evening, Mr. Devlin.'

They were in the *salon*. Peter had been the perfect guest and Berthe the perfect hostess. Chantal had been placed next to him at the table. She had automatically escorted him into the *salon* and without very much trouble placed herself next to him on a brocade sofa.

Francesca had to be satisfied with Julien's attentions, although she could no longer pretend that it wasn't Peter's company she craved, and the sight of him with Chantal didn't anger her.

She wanted to tell him Chantal would make a terrible mother to his child but she knew it would be useless; when a man was blinded by a woman's natural charms, sense was disregarded.

The light came only from two strategically placed lamps which cast eerie shadows across the room. Francesca had come to the conclusion that it was done purposely to create the correct atmosphere.

Tonight Francesca had entered the dining-room to hear Berthe say, 'You will have to excuse my sister-in-law, Mr. Devlin. She is not well enough to be present this evening.'

As Peter had murmured a conventional reply, Francesca had felt slightly shocked. Only that afternoon Marguerite had been eagerly looking forward to meeting 'Chantal's young man' and seemed perfectly well.

This latest meeting with Marguerite had been less painful for Francesca, for Berthe and Chantal had been present too and Marguerite had addressed herself mainly to them. And apart from her obsession that Paul was alive she seemed quite normal.

'There must be a ghost too,' Peter went on a moment later. 'I should think you have an ancestor who haunts the corridors of the château.'

'No, I'm afraid we haven't,' answered Berthe. 'It is most disappointing, is it not?' She gave a little laugh. 'We often think it is a pity, but it is often said that to see ghosts it is necessary to be of an imaginative nature. We Varonnes have our roots too close to the soil to possess good imaginations. But it is true that those, like yourself, Mr. Devlin, who are not used to places like this and who wish to see a ghost, do tend to let the atmosphere affect them.'

He stirred his coffee thoughtfully and then sat back. 'There is also a theory I've heard that only certain people are receptive to ghosts.'

'Do you mean that a ghost could appear in this very room and only one of us see it?' Julien asked politely.

'It has been known,' answered Peter, 'although I don't entirely believe it could be due to Madame Varonne's theory.'

'It has never happened in this château, Mr. Devlin,' said Berthe.

'You can't possibly know, Madame Varonne. Someone, at some time, might have passed a person in one of the corridors — a ghost — without realising it wasn't a human being at all. Ghosts, I recall, often only materialise to the one person who meant something to them in life.'

Berthe gave a derogatory laugh. 'If that is so, Mr. Devlin, the fact has never been recorded.'

'Perhaps,' said Francesca quietly, 'that is what ails Maman.'

Berthe looked at her sharply. 'What nonsense. And it is most cruel to say such things about poor Marguerite.'

Chantal shuddered expressively and pushed herself closer to Peter. 'Oh, please stop talking of ghosts, or I won't sleep a wink tonight.'

She looked up at him appealingly and he smiled down at her. 'Poor Chantal. Are you so afraid of the dark? Who would have thought it?'

Berthe gave another of her short, nervous laughs and said in a deliberate attempt to change the subject, 'What have you been doing since you arrived at St. Marcel, Mr. Devlin?'

'I've been visiting châteaux. I went to Mayneau the day before yesterday. It was very interesting. I'm very interested in old buildings.'

'Is that why you came to St. Marcel, Mr. Devlin?' It was Julien who had spoken.

Francesca cast him a sideways glance. In the discreet light shed by the shaded lamps he did look like Paul. He had the same colouring, a similar build; the same sleek, well-fed appearance.

'Partly. Do-as-you-please holidays always attract me. I like the fishing and the scenery too. I hate jostling for a place on the beach.

'I'd very much like to look over this

place too, if I may,' he said, looking at Berthe again.

Berthe took his cup and refilled it, and as she handed it back she said, 'I don't think you would find it of particular interest, Mr. Devlin. Many of our treasures have been sold over the years to pay for one disaster or another. Many were stolen by the Germans during the last war, and were never recovered. We would love to replenish them, but you no doubt know the price that paintings and antiques fetch nowadays as well as we do. We just couldn't afford it.'

'Have you been to Monbazillac?' Julien asked. 'It is certainly worth a visit.'

'Thank you,' answered Peter. 'I will make a note of it.'

Francesca noticed that Chantal was still sitting against him, her thigh against his. Peter did not seem disposed towards moving away.

'The château dates from the late sixteenth century,' she said, pleased at being able to disclose this little piece of information.

'There are probably some very interesting nooks and crannies,' he went on, slowly savouring Madame Resaque's excellent coffee. 'I wouldn't mind claiming privilege and asking to explore them.'

'You would need someone to guide you, Peter,' giggled Chantal.

'Naturally.'

Berthe Varonne cleared her throat. Francesca, for how little she had spoken to him this evening, might not have bothered with her careful toilette.

She had brought out a long evening dress of emerald green silk. Its high neckline and long sleeves contrasted spectacularly with Chantal's dress which revealed a great deal of its wearer.

For the first time since Paul's death Francesca had felt the urge to look good. Her hair had been washed and set, and brushed until it did, indeed, look like spun silver. Only in this light she looked prematurely grey. The dress was an expensive one and the price showed in its elegant cut which ensured its fit despite her loss of weight. The only jewellery she wore was a pair of earrings — semi-precious beryls set in gold filigree. Paul had bought them on their last anniversary a month before he died.

For the first time since then she felt feminine and attractive, but she might not have troubled. He hadn't noticed.

She looked down at her hands. The chased gold wedding ring she still wore looked enormous on her slim finger and the skin was almost transparent over her bones.

'Chantal will be pleased to show you around, Mr. Devlin,' Berthe said in a thoughtful voice. 'Perhaps you and she would make arrangements for a suitable day and time.'

Peter put his empty cup down on the table. 'Why not now?'

Berthe laughed. 'Oh, that is impossible, I'm afraid. It would be a very good atmosphere though, would it not? But unfortunately the greater part of the château is in disuse, some parts a little dangerous too, and most important, there is no electricity in the unused part. You would see nothing at all, Mr. Devlin.'

Slowly she poured more coffee into her own cup. 'Francesca tells me you work for your government.' Francesca thought she was making a deliberate attempt to change the subject again. 'Are you a translator? Chantal tells me your French is perfect.'

'Among other things, *madame*.'

Francesca stared at him. This urbane Englishman, uttering meaningless pleasantries, was hardly the same person she had been with only yesterday. The loss of that intimacy was like a gnawing hunger inside her. Suddenly she could sit there no longer and watch Chantal snuggle up against him, and suffer Peter being politely cool towards her.

She put her cup down. It clattered onto the table. 'I think I'll look in on Maman,' she said.

They all looked at her. It was as if

they had just remembered her presence. The look on their faces, white in the half-light, gave her a crazy urge to laugh.

Instead she said, 'I don't think I'll come back. It's getting late so I'll say my goodnights to you all now.' She encompassed Peter in the tight smile she flashed them all.

It wasn't their fault she had nothing to say. It was the château and its atmosphere; it seemed to sap all her personality, leaving only a shell.

'There's no need to go to Marguerite,' Berthe said quickly. 'I looked in on her before we came in for dinner and she was already asleep. She'll sleep soundly until morning, and Jeanne goes in from time to time.'

Francesca did not answer and Berthe said in a bright voice. 'It was so good of you, Mr. Devlin, to take Francesca out yesterday. The moment I saw her come in I could see the difference the outing had made. But I warned her — didn't I, Francesca? She mustn't exert herself too much. Illnesses, whether they are physical or mental, take a great deal of getting over.'

Francesca murmured 'Good night' again and walked slowly to the door. The frequency her recent illness was mentioned, it was as if they wanted her to be unbalanced, or they wanted Peter to believe it. As she went she was aware that Peter, who had risen also, was watching her too.

Once she had closed the door the buzz of conversation started up again, in French this time, but she didn't doubt they were only uttering the same kind of vagaries.

The remaining Varonnes were a tightly-knit family, sufficient unto themselves. They neither desired nor wanted visitors. It depressed Francesca unreasonably to realise that Chantal must be very keen on Peter, and her parents anxious for a match, for this invitation to have been issued tonight.

The memory of Julien's sudden appearance at the end of the darkened corridor only yesterday made her shiver a little as she went towards Marguerite's room. Even in a long-sleeved dress, on a summer evening, the corridors of the château were chilly. A far cry from a small centrally heated flat she was used to.

Only one light was left burning in the corridor. She searched for a switch so she could flood the place with searching light, but could find none. Although she had no real reason to hesitate, Francesca walked rather slowly towards her mother-in-law's room.

She stopped halfway along the corridor, foolishly peering into the gloom ahead, as if she expected an apparition to appear. Her heart thudded unevenly at the sound of a faint scratching nearby. Sheer will power alone urged her on to investigate and she almost laughed out loud in relief at the sight of Ninon's pathetic attempts to gain entry into Marguerite's room.

'Hush, Ninon,' she whispered. '*Madame* is asleep. You mustn't wake her, or they'll blame me.' Ninon looked up at Francesca, hopefully, brushing against the long skirt of her evening dress.

Francesca crouched down and stroked her fur gently. 'You probably haven't understood one word I've spoken to you.' Ninon purred and Francesca gave a little laugh. 'It doesn't matter, does it, *chérie*? We understand each other well enough. Words aren't necessary between us.'

She straightened up. She knocked gently on the door and listened carefully. The door was stout, like all the others in the château, and hewn from solid oak. But Francesca was sure she heard someone stir from within the room; an almost indiscernible scrape of chair legs on stone. Francesca felt herself stiffen. Then she recovered almost immediately. She remembered the psychiatrist at the nursing home saying, 'I can help you, Francesca,' when she had vehemently insisted that she had not been imagining things, 'but you must help yourself.'

Soon she had come to understand that it was easy to believe a figment of the imagination is real, but no more would she allow her wild imaginings to haunt her life.

As gently as she could she turned the handle and opened the door. To her dismay Ninon streaked into the room and Francesca chided herself silently for not holding on to the animal.

She stood in thc doorway. One shaded lamp by the bedside was alight. In the huge bed the frail figure of Marguerite lay sleeping.

As Francesca stood immobile by the door her own heartbeats was the only noise she could hear, yet she felt her skin prickle slightly. She was so sure she had heard someone moving around. Surely Marguerite hadn't the guile to pretend.

She crossed quickly to the bed. The rise and fall of Marguerite's chest was as gentle as a bird's.

'Maman,' Francesca said softly. There was no response. If Marguerite was pretending, she was a good actress.

Francesca turned away, searching for Ninon in the darkness beyond the pool of light shed by the lamp. She spotted her a moment later, scratching against the heavy velvet curtains. She quickly scooped the cat into her arms and carried her from the room before Marguerite could be disturbed.

When she reached the head of the stairs Peter and Chantal were at the bottom. One of Chantal's hands was on his shoulder, her face close to his. They were both talking in whispers, in French. Like lovers.

Dismay stabbed into her as she watched them. I'm jealous, she thought in alarm.

Just then Berthe and Julien came up to the couple, and Peter broke away. They had come out of the library, bringing with them a book which they pressed onto Peter.

Francesca, still unseen at the head of the stairs, found her lips curving into a smile. It would hardly need the two of them to find one book. How tactful they were in allowing the couple to make their farewells in private.

Peter was shaking Julien's hand, thanking them for the evening, promising to see them again before he left.

It was a cosy scene and Francesca felt that there was no place in it for her. She let Ninon go and turned to go back to her room.

It was a long time before she began to undress, although she couldn't remember what thoughts had passed through her mind while she sat tensely on the edge of her bed.

She did know that she wasn't capable of coping with this sudden attraction to Peter Devlin. Before her marriage to Paul she had known few men; now alone again at twenty-three Francesca found that she was as dangerously vulnerable as any teenager having a first infatuation.

Common sense told her he only pitied her, and because of his own experience wanted to help her. For him the real appeal lay in Chantal's charm. Chantal whose attraction few men could resist. And even that he would forget once he was back in England again.

Each time Francesca had seen Peter she had been in some kind of trouble, and each time, out of kindness, he took pity on her. He was a kind man. Kind. How Paul would have used that description as an insult.

Slowly she took off her dress and wrapped herself in a dressing-gown. She was still in a thoughtful mood when she began to brush her hair. She smiled at her own reflection; it was odd how childhood habits remained. Nowadays she still found the rhythmic action soothing.

Suddenly she stopped, the brush raised above her head. The door at the end of the corridor had slammed shut. Francesca hurried across to her own door and opened it slightly. She would have gone out into the corridor, only she hesitated behind her door at the sound of whispered voices in the corridor.

She heard Chantal's unmistakable giggle, followed by a gasp, and 'Non, non, chéri, Francesca . . . '

The rest of the sentence was lost as the door closed and Francesca heard nothing more than two people laughing, one laugh that was Chantal's and another that was definitely masculine.

Francesca closed her own door quickly then and sank back against it. So that was what they were whispering about in the hall, she thought. They were arranging this sordid little rendezvous. A formal good night and a return by way of the tower door later.

She was shaking uncontrollably. Chantal made no secret of her own lack of morals, but such abuse of Julien and Berthe's hospitality on Peter's part disgusted her. There was no doubt of Chantal's power over any man, but Peter's behaviour disappointed her; she so wanted to believe him above sordid little intrigues.

What do I know of any man? she asked herself angrily as she gathered up her towel and soapbag. After five years of marriage I couldn't even claim to know the man who was my husband.

She crept across the hall to the bathroom as if it were she who were the transgressor. Illogically she felt that she would die of shame if Peter came out of Chantal's room now. If she didn't actually meet him face to face she could, at least, try to pretend that she didn't know.

When she came back she was still angry, although towards whom it was directed Francesca wasn't quite sure. A little towards them all she supposed, towards herself most of all. She didn't want to be vulnerable any more, and meeting Peter Devlin had proved that she was.

She went across to Chantal's door. No sound came from within the room now. Her hands clenched at her sides as she resisted the impulse to beat at it, to shock them as she had been shocked.

She stood like that for a few moments and then, sadly, she went back to her room.

★ ★ ★

Her sleep was shallow, her dreams many. When she awoke it was with a start. The first feeble fingers of early morning light were creeping through the shutters. Francesca lay there a moment before realising that it was the closing of the tower door that had awoken her. It was well-oiled, in constant use, yet the way the wind blew around the corner ensured a constant draught to prevent it closing quietly.

Her ears strained for the sound of his car, but none came. Francesca pulled the covers up over her ears and at last fell into a deep sleep.

It was well into the morning when she awoke again. No one but Jeanne was around when Francesca went into *petit dejeuner*. The table was laid for breakfast, for the Varonnes, contrary to

French custom, enjoyed a cooked breakfast, but a freshly baked roll was all Francesca could manage, and then it was with the greatest difficulty.

Jeanne informed her that Madame and Monsieur had gone into Perigeaux and would not be back until after lunch, and Marguerite was still in her room. Francesca was glad not to disturb her, happier still not to have to face Berthe and Julien this morning.

However, it was, to Francesca, the greatest misfortune to have chosen to come out of the breakfast-room the exact moment that Chantal was coming along the corridor. She wore a cardigan slung across her shoulders over a low-cut cotton dress. The sight of her sauntering along, swinging her handbag gaily as she walked, revived all Francesca's feelings of anger and jealousy.

'*Bonjour*, Francesca,' she said gaily. 'It is a good morning once more I see.'

'You had a good night too, I think,' retorted Francesca.

Chantal admired her reflection in a

large, gilt-mounted mirror on the wall. 'It was very enjoyable. It isn't very often that we have visitors. It gets very lonely for me as you can well imagine.'

'I doubt that, Chantal.' Her tone was so sharp that Chantal's eyes narrowed in amazement and curiosity. 'Do your parents' guests usually come back through the side entrance?'

Chantal looked at her blankly. *'Pardon?'*

Francesca hated herself. She was giving way to anger and jealousy she had no right to feel. A girl of eighteen was able to do as she pleased, and so was Peter Devlin.

'Don't pretend you don't know what I'm talking about, Chantal. I'm not a fool, whatever you and your parents would like to believe. I heard Peter come back last night after everyone else was in bed.'

For a moment Chantal looked astounded and then she smiled slyly, leaning back against the stair rail. 'So?'

'I'm not particularly interested in

your morals. Chantal, but I do object to your carrying on an affair under your parents' roof. Haven't you any moral conscience at all?'

Chantal continued to smile. 'You are very concerned about my parents, Francesca. It is very commendable but they are quite aware of my weaknesses.'

Francesca smiled scornfully. 'I doubt it. Parents tend to view their offspring through rose-coloured spectacles.'

'But only remember the circumstances of my birth, Francesca. I am what might be called the cuckoo in this nest. Fidelity is not part of the Varonne family motto, and has never been part of their way of life.'

She viewed Francesca from under her dark lashes. Inside her Francesca fought an impotent fury. 'Do you really think a man like Peter Devlin has any real interest in you, Chantal?'

Chantal tossed back her hair. 'I really don't care. It's only a pity you do.' Her smile became scornful. 'He likes me for what I am. What is wrong with that? I am gay and good fun to be with. I make a man happy. I am good at making men happy.'

'You are so very young, Chantal.' But the way Chantal was smiling at her made Francesca feel that it was she who was very young and Chantal ages old.

All of a sudden her anger melted. 'Don't you realise how foolish your behaviour is?'

Chantal laughed. 'It is you who are the fool, dear Francesca, not I, if you pretend to yourself that I would want your idea of morality. You are a hypocrite and I can tell you if I had been older Paul would never have married you. I know all about you. He has told me and I know he couldn't love you. It's me he loved because you couldn't possibly make him happy. You had no notion of how to make him happy . . .'

'Chantal!'

The girl stopped. She straightened up. 'Please don't moralise to me, dear cousin,' she said as she started down the stairs. 'Behind that cool English manner, the sorrowing widow has, herself, a penchant for Mr. Peter Devlin.'

She laughed maddeningly and ran lightly down the rest of the stairs, leaving a furious Francesca behind. When she reached the bottom she waved and laughed again, 'I shall give Peter your love, Francesca!'

After Chantal had gone Francesca turned away and went towards Marguerite's room. Marguerite no longer held any terrors for her. These people had so many fears and weaknesses they could only make Francesca feel strong.

Jeanne was just coming out of the room. She smiled at Francesca, and in her usual manner then looked down at the floor respectfully until Francesca had gone inside.

Marguerite was sitting at her dressing-table carefully making up her face and Ninon was curled across her knee. When Francesca came in the cat silently jumped to the floor and ran up to her. For once

Francesca ignored her and Ninon ran back.

'*Bonjour*, Francesca,' Marguerite beamed through her mirror. 'How nice to see you.'

Francesca smiled stiffly. She found that her hands were clenched together tensely and deliberately she drew them apart.

'Sit down. Sit down,' urged Marguerite as she patted powder onto her pale cheeks using a wisp of swansdown.

Francesca did as she was bid and sat down in a brocaded chair, resting her hands on its arms. 'I wondered if you were recovered this morning, Maman. You must be disappointed to have missed the dinner party last night.'

'I feel wonderful. I had a good night's rest. I wanted to come, of course, because I was longing to meet Chantal's young man. Berthe tells me he is delightful. I only hope Chantal doesn't spoil things. She is, Francesca, quite frankly a flirt. If this man is as Berthe says she will frighten him away.'

'I don't think Peter Devlin is the right man for Chantal,' Francesca said coldly. 'I wouldn't be too hopeful if I were you, Maman. He is just on holiday. He will go back and forget her.'

She spoke more for her own satisfaction than to inform Marguerite.

Marguerite gave a slight shrug. 'That is a pity, but it cannot be helped. Still, I would have liked to have met him, Francesca. We get so few visitors here since . . . ' She twisted round on the stool. 'Now let me look at *you*. How are you, my child?'

'I'm fine, Maman.'

'Yes, you look it now. It was as I said; once you were here, eating Madame Resaque's food and being looked after properly by us. It was only a pity you couldn't have been in a French nursing home . . . '

Francesca broke in impatiently, 'I came here to enquire after *you*, Maman.'

Marguerite looked surprised. 'But I told you, I am fine.'

Francesca looked at her steadily. 'I

came in after dinner to see you, but you were fast asleep.'

Marguerite smiled foolishly. 'How thoughtful you are, *chérie*. You are a good, kind girl. Berthe said I looked tired. I don't always realise it myself and she is usually right. She brought me a glass of malted milk and that always gives me a sound night's sleep. You should try it if you ever find you cannot sleep.'

'I will,' answered Francesca gently.

Marguerite removed the plastic cape she wore around her shoulders while making-up. Every inch the Frenchwoman even in sickness, Francesca thought. She was becoming fond of her mother-in-law in a pitying kind of way. It was a shame that it was too late for a real friendship.

'I hope you gave my apologies to our guest, Francesca. He must have thought me extremely rude.'

'He understood.'

'Berthe said he would,' Marguerite said happily.

Francesca's hand tightened on the arms of her chair. 'Maman, I may be going back to England soon . . . '

Marguerite had crossed the room and was carefully selecting a dress from the wardrobe. She clutched one to her as she swung round. 'Going back! So soon. But you have come to stay. Paul isn't going with you is he, Francesca? This isn't his idea, is it?'

Francesca smiled again. 'No, Maman. You will have him all to yourself while I'm gone, so don't pretend that you'll be sorry.'

Marguerite's face stiffened. 'No, I will not pretend. I never wanted him to marry as you know, and if he had to, well, he was a Varonne; the name still means something. I wanted him to marry well, and from here. But he chose you and England. I confess I could never understand why.'

Francesca's hands clenched convulsively in her lap. 'But now you are a Varonne and you are here where you belong. I have welcomed you here because you are my son's choice and you bear our name. You are as a daughter to me now.' Her eyes glittered and Francesca felt a stirring of fear. She had no idea Marguerite's devotion to the family cause was so fanatical. 'So you must say no more of going back to England. If you dislike France you should never have married a Frenchman. You should be honoured to be here, to be one of us.'

Just now Marguerite sounded distressingly sane; she was more like the woman Francesca remembered. It would be useless to tell her Paul never intended to live in France.

'When I came here, Maman, I left quite a number of matters outstanding, matters that must be dealt with — disposing of the lease to the flat for instance.' She had seized on the first excuse she could think of. 'Paul . . . ' she almost choked, 'hasn't had the time to go back to attend to these things.'

Marguerite Varonne's face relaxed. She closed the wardrobe door almost silently and turned back to face Francesca. 'Yes, I should have realised this. But you mustn't go just yet. Surely you don't have to? All this travelling to and fro cannot be good for you. Promise me you will wait a little longer.'

Francesca sighed. As a person Marguerite despised her; as a Varonne she was entitled to her concern.

'All right, Maman,' she answered. 'I will leave it a little longer.'

8

Francesca escaped as soon as she could. With Chantal out and Berthe and Julien away until the afternoon, she was virtually free, and it was a heady sensation. Once outside the château she could discard her heavy woollen jacket and let the sun seep into her bones.

What to do with her few precious hours of freedom was the problem now. Roaming the château corridors was not an attractive proposition, neither was staying with Marguerite.

She knew she could take the car out, but she was reluctant to go to the village, for whenever she did she always met Peter, and Peter was the last person she wanted to see this morning. Last night was still too fresh in her mind. And yet if she did not see him she would know he was with Chantal. Better not to go.

She walked across the terrace and sat down on the parapet. Down below the workers toiled like industrious bees in the vineyard amongst the ripening grapes, and still further away she could see the red roofs of St. Marcel and the glint of the sun on the river.

All was peaceful out here — idyllic, yet inside the château the very air seemed filled with unease.

Paul and I could have been happy here, she thought. If only we had come before the château was steeped into silent mourning for its last son.

She looked up at its ivy-strewn walls, at the family crest. The creeper had almost encroached upon it. Soon the stone phoenix would have disappeared for good behind the ivy. Francesca wondered if anyone would trouble to cut back the clinging tentacles, but doubted that they would, and the phoenix would soon be gone for ever.

The tower windows gazed sightlessly down into the valley. From them predators coud be seen approaching from miles away. Her eyes scanned one and then the other and she froze into immobility at the flicker of movement behind it.

She jumped to her feet and started towards the tower, but stopped in her tracks at the sound of an approaching car. Elation, anger, dread put all else from her mind as Peter's familiar cream-coloured Citroen came towards her.

When she looked up at the tower window again there was nothing to be seen. A bird passing by, she thought, or a strand of ivy blown across in the breeze.

She turned back just as Peter got out of the car. He looked impossibly fresh and innocent, wearing a pale blue pullover and a pair of fawn slacks.

'Hi,' he said, giving her a smile of greeting.

She made no move to go to him. Instead she stood with her hands in her skirt pockets and said coldly, 'Chantal has gone out.'

She smiled then to herself. Chantal had gone out to meet him; he had come here to see Chantal. And they had missed each other.

He was nonplussed. He smiled with an ease that did nothing to soothe her anger and hurt. 'Yes, and Julien and Berthe are in Perigeaux.' She gave him a sharp look.

'Elementary, my dear Francesca; they told me last night.' His voice softened. 'I came to see you.'

Liar, she thought.

She walked back to the edge of the terrace and gazed down, for the want of something else to do. Seeing him was more embarrassing than she had imagined it would be. She felt he had betrayed her, which was nonsense, for there was nothing between them. And yet the pain was intense. She had trusted him.

He came across to stand by her side. 'Great view, isn't it?'

'Originally there was a castle on this site and it had to be as impregnable as possible.'

'It still is, I should say.'

She glanced up at him but he was gazing out into the valley. Then he looked down at her and grinned. It was a faintly lopsided grin and very appealing.

She looked away again quickly. 'It was a bit grim last night, wasn't it?' he said.

'What do you mean?'

'The Varonnes acting in the grand manner. I felt as though I should touch my forelock.'

'Oh, that. It's all their inbred pride in the tradition of the family. *It's rubbish*,' she added vehemently.

He put his hand on her shoulder but she shrugged it off, unable to bear him touching her now. 'You are grumpy this morning, aren't you, Francesca?' he said lightly. 'I'm willing to bet you're not long from your bed. I'm just the same, you know. I'm usually unbearable before noon.'

She gave a broken little laugh and he went on, 'But I have something that will put the smile back on your face. Pasquale's wife is just about the most obliging woman one could wish to meet. She's packed the freshest ham rolls you'll ever eat, some very pungent cheese, local plonk and some rather succulent peaches — and there's enough for two.'

He was so sure of her she could have screamed.

'Come on, Francesca, let's go.'

'No!'

He had already started towards the car, but the vehemence in her voice brought him up sharply. 'But you don't even know where we're going.'

'I don't care.'

He came back to her. This time she didn't bother to shake off the arm he pressed around her shoulders. 'It will do you good to get away from here for a while, Francesca. You might even find that one of your bad days has turned into one of your good ones.'

'You're very persuasive, Peter,' she said truthfully, allowing him to lead her towards the car, 'but then I was always easily led.'

He glanced at her. She knew he was puzzled as well he might be. He could have no real idea what lay behind her coldness towards him. Neither could he know it was masking an explosive anger.

Once they were in the car he let off the handbrake and allowed the car to coast silently through the gateway.

'You look as if you're having some very fierce thoughts,' he said, smiling at her slightly. He spoke lightly, but behind it was anxiety.

'Do you really want to know what I'm thinking?'

'I'm fascinated.'

'I was thinking about my marriage. Paul wasn't faithful to me.'

His smile faded. 'Who has put that little piece of malice into your head?'

'Strangely enough, no one. I didn't even realise it until I came here. I don't know why not. Paul wasn't the kind of man to be faithful to one woman. He liked women and they liked him.'

'You told me he wasn't the type of man to consider making a will, yet he did.'

'This is different.'

'You're imagining things, Francesca. If you didn't realise it in five years of living with the man, why start now? You couldn't possibly know.'

'But I do.'

'Don't torture yourself, Francesca,' he pleaded, and to her surprise he sounded genuinely concerned. 'You can do yourself no good by thinking about it now because you'll never know.'

'I'm not torturing myself,' she answered truthfully. 'I'm just facing some long overdue facts about Paul.'

He appeared to be about to say something more, but she forestalled him by asking, 'Where are we going?'

'To eat our lunch by the river first. Then to Château Ceyranne. It isn't far from here, but, unlike Varonne, it is open to the public and has a great many treasures on view. It may not be madly exciting, but it's somewhere to go on a beautiful sunny day like this.'

'I thought you did find old buildings 'madly exciting',' she said, glancing across at him.

He grinned again. 'I was thinking of it from your point of view.'

'It sounds nice,' she murmured, trying to sound enthusiastic, but failing miserably. She hated Chantal more than ever for spoiling one of the best relationships she'd had with anyone for a long time. Hating herself too for being woman enough to want even more than the friendship he was willing to give.

They slowed as they came to the village; Francesca's apathy was suddenly dispersed at the sight of a man who was toiling up one of the steep, cobbled streets towards them. It was the man who had bumped into her at Bordeaux.

She sat up straight. 'Peter. That man! He was at Bordeaux and he's been staying in St. Marcel all week!'

Peter looked at her and frowned.

'He's staying at the hotel. His name is François Montcalm.'

'You know him?' she asked in amazement.

'Well, yes. As I said, he's staying at the hotel. He has a room on the same floor as mine. Sometimes we share a table at breakfast. He's on holiday too. Why are you so surprised?'

'Because he's here too. Coincidence I suppose.'

'He stayed at Perigeaux for a couple of days after he arrived but he didn't like his hotel and moved here. As a matter of fact he's told me of quite a few interesting places to visit.'

As the car drew level Peter stopped. The man stopped too, looking startled as if he had only just seen them.

'Francois,' said Peter, 'allow me to introduce you to Madame Varonne.'

The man gave her a dour smile and bowed stiffly over her hand. '*Enchanté, madame.*'

'Madame Varonne lives in the château I visited yesterday, Francois.'

'You are most fortunate,' said Francois Montcalm, giving her another smile. 'It has a fascinating look about it.'

Peter looked at Francesca. 'Francois was quite green with envy when I had my invitation to dinner. He's mad about old buildings.'

'We met at Bordeaux I recall,' said Francesca.

The man frowned. 'I do not recall, *madame*.'

Francesca smiled. 'I'm not surprised. You bumped into me. I don't think you even looked at me at the time.'

'Ah yes, now I do recall bumping into a lady, but I was in a hurry.'

Now Francesca laughed. 'Isn't everyone at airports?'

Peter took off the handbrake again. He waved to the man, ' 'Bye, Francois.'

'I'm happy to have made your acquaintance, *madame*,' he said, taking Francesca's hand momentarily and then stepping back.

'Quaint manners these continentals

have,' said Peter as they left the village behind. He glanced at her speculatively. 'It bowls the girls over every time. But he's a nice chap. We've become quite friendly since he came.'

'He doesn't look the friendly sort to me,' she answered thoughtfully.

'The French are reserved despite their reputation. He is very friendly in his own language.'

They had their picnic lunch near the river at Ceyranne where tall poplars lined the banks of the river and carts drawn by yoked oxen toiled in the fields on the opposite bank.

Peter kept up a constant flow of conversation, telling her about the places he'd visited and the characters he had met. Francesca envied him his ability to make friends so easily.

The food was as appetising as Peter had promised it would be, but she ate little. She blamed her lack of enthusiasm on a late breakfast and he remarked, 'Me too.'

Finally she did manage a respectable

lunch and sat back to enjoy a cigarette afterwards. He tidied away what remained of their meal and she allowed him to do it. When he had finished he came to sit cross-legged in front of her.

He gazed at her for a few moments and Francesca, aware of it, kept on looking across the fields.

'Hadn't you better tell me what I've done to annoy you?'

Her eyes opened wide. She turned her head slowly to look at him. She was convinced she had been behaving quite normally since they left the château.

'What do you mean?'

'Only you can tell me that,' he answered and his gaze on her face was unwavering. 'There can only be yesterday evening, and I refuse to believe you're so petty as to resent my not being at your side constantly, or has something upset you again that has nothing to do with me?'

'You're mistaken.'

'No, I'm not. I'm very sensitive to your moods, Francesca. I mean to know so the sooner you tell me the quicker it will be over.'

She crushed out her cigarette. 'I was brought up by elderly people. I was married young, almost straight from school, and Paul sheltered me too. You could say I'm rather narrow-minded . . .'

'Well?'

'You're not making it easy for me.'

'You're making it damned impossible for me to understand what you're talking about,' he said angrily.

She looked at him. 'You didn't leave it late enough to come back last night; I was still awake and I heard you go into Chantal's room.'

His eyes flickered but his gaze didn't waver. 'I see, but Chantal is still a child.'

'She's eighteen,' Francesca snapped, 'and a woman. I was married at that age.'

'You aren't Chantal,' he said softly, and then a moment later, 'Look, Francesca, I'm sure you heard someone go to Chantal's room last night. There are few able young men in the village whose manhood hasn't been proven by a visit to Chantal in her room in the dead of night. She has, you might say, something of a reputation in the village, and people talk. But I'm not a village youth and I proved my manhood years ago.'

'It wasn't you?'

'No, and,' he added coldly, 'whoever it was can consider himself honoured. From what I've heard, since your husband died, mourning at the château has been absolute. Chantal has done little to encourage nocturnal visits. Pasquale's son was in love with her, and up until then he believed she was in love with him. Now she'll have nothing to do with him in that way. She is, as they say in popular songs, driving him mad.'

Francesca felt choked. Her joy was ruined by remorse. She pulled at a blade of grass, hardly daring to look at him. 'I'm sorry, Peter. Even if it had been you it was none of my business.'

'It was a logical conclusion to come to, although I can hardly admit to being flattered. I'd be the first to admit that Chantal can be dazzling, but I'm thirty-five years old. I'm not a callow youth to be bewitched by an adolescent with slightly more than her fair share of natural attributes and a sense of dress that would better suit an act in a third rate Parisian nightclub. And before you start to feel sorry for her, I can assure you she feels nothing for me. Like any man she meets, I'm just a challenge. My taste runs to something far more subtle, and, besides, my affections are already engaged elsewhere.'

'Oh,' she said, keeping her voice as steady as she could, 'who is she?'

'Come here and I'll tell you.'

She still didn't look at him for fear that he would see her eyes misting with tears. He reached over and brushed a fly away from her hair. 'You're jealous aren't you?' he said in an amused voice as the back of his hand touched her cheek and stayed there. 'You have no need to be, you know. No need at all.'

She closed her eyes and caught his hand, keeping it there, close to her cheek. 'Don't play games with me, Peter.'

'I don't like playing games. I've never been very good at them.'

A moment later his arms were around her and she was giving herself up to his kisses with a heart full of joy. He kissed her gently at first and then possessively, and her response was no less ardent.

'Why on earth did you think you had anything to fear from Chantal?' he murmured against her hair, and her answer was to pull him close again.

At last his hold on her loosened and she laid her head against his shoulder. For a moment neither spoke and then he said, 'We'd better go for our guided tour round the château.'

She looked across to the hill on which it was perched. It was old and historic like Varonne, but the sight of it didn't fill her with dread. She looked back at him and gave a little laugh. 'Do we have to go in?'

'I think we should,' he said seriously, 'or I might forget all my scruples and take you back to the hotel instead.'

'I'd rather do that,' she said softly.

He made no attempt to move away from her, but suddenly the softness left his eyes and despite his closeness he was remote. 'No, Francesca. Not now. Not here.'

Her hands dropped into her lap and he said softly, 'There's a whole lifetime ahead.'

She looked up at him and smiled. 'Do you mean it?'

He kissed her again. 'I've waited for you a long time. I'm a patient man. I can wait a little longer, until you've said that final goodbye to Paul.'

She gasped and drew away. 'What are you trying to say?'

'That you haven't let him go yet. I understand. It's still too soon, Francesca. You're still too involved with him and his memory. I can wait until you've let him go, but I won't have you until you do.'

'Have you let Kaye go? You loved her, I know you did.'

'Yes, I did, and there'll always be a place for her in my heart. I won't pretend otherwise because it's as it should be, but you'll never have to doubt my feelings for you. You'll never be my second best. Don't ever think so. What I shared with Kaye is over and done with, but you're my today and tomorrow.'

'Paul is the past for me too, Peter.'

'No, Francesca, not yet. He was the only man in your life for five years; you can't blot that out completely. I've no intention of sharing you with a ghost and there's no chance of anything else while you stay at the château.'

She got to her knees and put her arms around his waist, laying her head against his chest. She could hear the steady beating of his heart.

'I envy you your happy memories, Peter. I envy you your ability to see so clearly.'

She drew away from him. 'I don't have those memories.' She looked up at him. 'I know now that I didn't love Paul; I've really known it for a long time. I worshipped him like an idol on a pedestal. When he died I tried to take comfort in the memories I knew I should have. I wanted to think about the happy times because we'd had a happy marriage. We never had an argument. Not a ripple ever ruffled the surface of our existence.'

She got to her feet and walked over to the water's edge to stare down at the river.

'He was the perfect husband. I adored him. We had friends, went to parties. Women flocked around him and I was envied. I liked that. What woman wouldn't? When he went abroad, as he often did, he never returned without a gift for me. I was the earth to his sun. The life we led was something that might have come out of a smart society column in a newspaper, the clothes he chose for me might have come from the pages of *Vogue*. Nothing but the best — always.'

'Are you trying to tell me you were unhappy?'

She turned to face him. Her eyes grew round. 'I didn't know what unhappiness was, Peter. Not until he died. And then I started to think back, trying to recall the little things we shared together, to gain comfort from them. I couldn't. There was nothing. We shared nothing. Our marriage was so totally different to any other I knew, and I hadn't even thought about it in five years. We were just two people who had lived together all that time. When he'd gone it was as if I'd lived with a stranger; I couldn't even remember what he looked like with any clarity. I felt as though we'd been acting in a play, and now the play was over they'd taken the scenery away.'

She rubbed her arms, feeling suddenly cold although the sun was blazing down. 'That's what really tore me apart, Peter, nothing else. And that's when my trouble started. At the nursing home the psychiatrist gave it a name I couldn't even pronounce. It amounted to a subconscious guilt complex.'

He walked across the short distance to where she was standing and she went into his arms, standing there, comforted by his closeness as nothing else could comfort her.

One hand gently stroked her hair, 'We'll have good memories, Francesca,' he said into her hair.

'We've started already,' she answered in a choked voice.

She felt purified by her confession. The act of telling him of what had been buried deep inside her for so long, had cleansed her utterly. She was glad it was done.

* * *

The château no longer held fear for her. As the car sped along, bringing her nearer to it she could only be happy because he was by her side.

Château Ceyranne had been absorbing because Peter was with her. He kept his arm around her during their tour of the building and he translated into English whatever the guide had said. The château had a proud history as illustrated by the priceless tapestries, antiques and pictures. Perhaps now she would even find Varonne interesting. Happiness made all the difference.

He drove with both hands on the wheel but she was, nevertheless, close to him. It was a closeness that transcended the physical, a closeness of spirit Francesca knew she had never known before.

From time to time he glanced at her and smiled and just the sight of his smile made her wonder if anyone had ever known such happiness before.

'Do you think Diana will like me?' she asked him suddenly.

'Why not?' he answered, 'I do,' and she laughed.

'Won't Kaye's parents be hurt? Diana must mean a great deal to them.'

'She does. But they're nice people. They've been urging me to remarry for a long time now. They're not young and they realise Diana needs a settled home. They're not selfish; they'll be glad for us. How do you feel about taking on a ready-made family?'

'Supremely happy,' she answered truthfully. 'We can always add to, later on.'

His eyes grew round in mock surprice. 'My, my, aren't you ambitious?'

All too soon they came to the château and once more Francesca felt the power of its gloom on her mood. Peter drove right onto the terrace. He pulled her close again. 'You must leave here immediately, Francesca. I insist.'

'You're very impatient,' she teased.

He looked down at her and she thrilled at the tenderness she saw in his eyes. 'More than you can imagine,' he answered as he dropped a kiss on her forehead.

'Seriously though, Peter,' she told him, 'I'd leave here now if I could, but it's not right that I should. I've been here less than two weeks. What can I say to them? 'Sorry but I've fallen in love and I'm going now. So long.' I can't do it, Peter. It isn't fair. They have to live with Paul's death for the rest of their lives. I can afford to be with them a little longer even if it's only for Maman's sake. If she knew the truth she'd be shattered.'

The hardness of his expression was echoed in his voice. 'If they insist on acting out the tragedy for ever more, then let them. You're still young. You have a future, Francesca. Think of yourself.'

'That's no way to go through life. I know I can't live by that philosophy, Peter. It's best you should know that now. Whatever you say, I do owe them something.'

He gave a sigh of resignation and smiled a little as he fingered her hair. 'I wouldn't want you to be any different. I just couldn't bear you to be hurt any more.'

She put her hands up to cradle his

face. 'Darling, that's impossible now I have you.'

He pulled her to him and held her so tightly, for a moment she could hardly breathe. Then he kissed her fiercely before letting her go.

'Leave as soon as you can, Francesca. Let me know when and I'll make all the arrangements for the journey.'

She looked faintly surprised. 'Are you going to wait for me?'

He nodded. 'If I don't I'm afraid you might never come. Only don't make it too long.' His look of ferocity gave way to nonchalance. 'Chantal is a very persistent girl.'

She laughed and made to hit him but he parried the blow and kissed her again. 'As I said don't make it too long. My patience has its limits.'

Glancing at the château she said, 'I wish I could pack and go right now.' She looked at him again, 'Until I do, Peter, I think it might be best if you're not seen around the château.'

He nodded curtly. 'You know where I

can be reached if you need me.'

He was about to get out when she said, 'No, don't Peter.'

He caught her hand as she started to open the door and drew her back again. He kissed her quickly. 'That's just something on account.'

She grinned at him. Even the sight of the car disappearing around the corner wasn't enough to sour her new-found contentment. There was only a few days at the most to stay here and after that, a lifetime of happiness with Peter.

She stood at the edge of the terrace and watched the car tackle the tortuous bends until it was quite out of sight and, still smiling to herself, she went back to the château. She was halfway up the steps when quite suddenly she changed her mind, deciding to enter the château by way of the tower door. Julien and Berthe were sure to be back by now, Chantal also, and Francesca was very reluctant to meet any of them now. The happiness she felt must be all too clearly etched on her face and the knowledge of Peter's love was far too new and precious to be shared just yet. And just the thought of Marguerite filled her with what she knew was unnecessary guilt. To Marguerite she was still married to Paul and always would be.

The breeze that constantly blew round that corner was welcome. She shivered in delight as it ruffled her hair.

Ninon was lying in the sun in front of the door. When Francesca approached the cat jumped up and when she opened the door Ninon sprang up the stairs. Francesca expected to find her again on the half landing, waiting to be let into the main part of the château, but even though the door was firmly shut there was no sign of Ninon.

Francesca paused, glancing up the twisting stairs that led to the tower, and then without further hesitation she took the rest of the stairs two at a time. Her heels clattered loudly on the stone and, somehow, it was a reassuring sound.

But she hesitated again when she

came to the top, partly from breathlessness and partly from a new-born fear; a fear of what she would find behind the partially open door.

She told herself she was being ridiculous — fanciful.

There could be nothing behind that door but a disused room.

Quickly, she pushed open the door and stepped inside. Ninon was curled up on the bed, only the bed was not the straw pallet used by guards of years gone by; it was a modern divan and it was made up for use.

A newspaper lay negligently folded in a faded brocade armchair which bore the permanent imprint of occupancy in its seat. The coldness of the stone floor was tempered by a folk-weave rug. A wardrobe stood awkwardly in one of the rounded corners of the room, into which it could never properly fit.

Ninon purred with contentment and licked her paws while Francesca looked around her in amazement. This room was lighter and brighter than any she had yet seen in the château. There was a small dressing-table in another corner of the room and its mirror was cracked. On top of the dressing-table stood an ornate bottle, a bottle that Francesca recognised very well. She picked it up and turned it over in her hand. The smell was so potent it caught in Francesca's throat, making her feel slightly sick.

There was a sound from the door, a shadow fell across the dressing-table. The bottle slipped from Francesca's hand and clattered down onto the dressing-table.

'Berthe,' she said in a low frightened voice when she turned. 'You startled me coming in so quietly.'

Berthe Varonne glanced round. 'I did not hear you return,' she said unsmilingly. 'I wondered who it could be moving about up here.'

'The occupant perhaps,' she replied lightly.

'There is no occupant now.'

'But it was Paul.'

'Yes,' answered Berthe sinking down onto the divan. Absently she stroked Ninon. 'I had hoped you wouldn't come here. It must be distressing for you. Paul always slept here while he was in St. Marcel. Like a little boy he liked it up here. Afterwards we had to keep it as it was for Marguerite's sake. Sometimes she comes here too.'

Francesca looked at the cat. 'So does Ninon.'

'Animals cannot be told. Ninon was always more his cat than ours. When he was away she used to come up here and wait for him. She must still come looking for him . . . '

'Berthe,' Francesca said breathlessly, 'you must tell me. Is there something about Paul's death that you've been hiding from me?'

Berthe looked up. Her eyes were narrowed into slits so that Francesca could not read their expression. 'What can we be hiding from you? There is nothing.'

'I don't know, Berthe. It's just that since I've been here I've had the feeling there is something.'

Berthe sighed gently. 'There is nothing, but when you first came we wondered how to treat you. You had been in hospital . . . We did not know what was your frame of mind. We were used to being careful with Marguerite . . . '

'You thought I was mad,' she said in amazement.

'No, not mad, Francesca, but we were afraid. That is all.'

Francesca kept on looking at her. 'I'm leaving here soon, Berthe . . . '

To her surprise Berthe's eyes were brimming with tears. 'Leaving here? Surely not. You belong here.'

'No, I don't, Berthe. That is something you must all understand. It's only fair that I should be honest with you; I'm leaving here because I'm going to get married again.'

Berthe Varonne paled visibly. 'Married,' she said in a whisper. 'You said nothing of this before. How can it be so? Who is this man?'

'Peter Devlin. We've fallen in love.'

'Peter Devlin! Oh no, Francesca. Not him. You can't mean this. You can't be serious.'

'Oh, Berthe, I know you and Julien hoped that Chantal and Peter would . . . but it's impossible. There are many men for Chantal but only one for me.'

'But what about Paul?'

Francesca felt only anguish. 'Try to understand, Berthe,' she begged. 'For you Paul is the nephew you loved and lost. You can never replace him, but it's different for me; I have another chance. I don't want to spend the rest of my life alone.'

Berthe's drooping head jerked up. 'You don't have to.'

'This place is not for me. If I had a child — a Varonne — I might feel differently.'

'You must forgive my surprise,' Berthe said in a voice that was little more than a whisper. 'This is so unexpected.'

'Widows have been known to remarry,' Francesca said in a cold voice, resisting the human impulse to say *she* hadn't been unfaithful to her husband with a passing gypsy.

'Yes, of course, but . . . ' Her voice faded away.

Francesca walked across to the window. The view to the valley was magnificent. Even the terrace was far below, and the road was clearly visible like a curled white ribbon unfurling into the distance.

'I was a good wife to Paul, Berthe. In all our married life I never looked at another man in that way. And I never would if he'd lived. But he's dead and I'm twenty-three years old. I still have a long time ahead of me.'

She turned back to face Paul's aunt. 'Please try and be glad for me.'

'You have known him such a short time. Are you quite sure?'

'Very sure, Berthe.'

'It may only be loneliness, and you know nothing about him.'

'I know enough,' Francesca answered calmly. 'I am more capable of knowing my own mind than when I met Paul when I was eighteen.'

Berthe's eyes were still sad. 'Then you do love him.'

'Very much,' she answered and her cold heart was warmed at the very thought of it.

Berthe got to her feet slowly, like an old woman, almost too weary to make the effort. She put her arm around Francesca's shoulder. 'Francesca, I wish I knew what to say to you.'

'Just be glad for me. That's all I ask.'

Berthe straightened up. She walked towards the door and pulled it open. 'In future, Francesca, you'd better not wander around the château on your own. Some parts are unsafe.'

Francesca watched her go, feeling totally helpless and inadequate. She took one last look around the room. The sight of it was suddenly repugnant to her. She couldn't spend another moment in here. Dashing across the room she flung open the door, and didn't stop running until she had reached the sanctuary of her own room.

9

Dinner that night was the most uncomfortable meal Francesca had yet taken under that roof. Conversation was almost non-existent, the atmosphere strained, and it angered her a little to know that the matter had been discussed and her 'treachery' resented when they should be happy for her.

The whole of the table was once again in use although it could seat fivefold those present. Ritualistically the best china, the best glassware were in use, and the utilisation of candles exclusively for light, made the atmosphere more appressive than Francesca usually found it.

But for once she was glad of her mother-in-law's presence; it precluded any talk of Peter. Only Chantal, oddly enough, was in high spirits. Throughout the meal she gave Francesca sly smiles across the table and Francesca was glad to find Peter's theory correct. Chantal would not pine over any man.

As soon as she could Francesca made her excuses to go to her room. As she fled along the corridor nameless fears pursued her in the half light. The phoenix on the tapestry at the head of the stairs seemed to have a gleam of evil in its eye that Francesca hadn't noticed before.

She wished now that she hadn't asked Peter to stay away. Every nerve in her body cried out for the comfort of his presence and the reassurance only he could give her. But it was completely dark out there just now and the thought of driving down through that impenetrable blanket of blackness to the village to see him was unbearable.

Tomorrow, Francesca decided, she would go to see him, and he would make immediate arrangements for their return to London.

As she lay sleepless in her bed she heard the familiar thud of the tower door closing. Her body went rigid as footsteps came slowly down the corridor. Someone paused outside her room and like a child afraid of the dark, Francesca buried her head beneath the covers and whoever had passed, went on.

Soon, she promised herself, soon this would only be a vague memory; a bad dream to be dispersed in the morning of a new love.

* * *

The following morning, gratefully, Francesca ate her breakfast alone and was able to go straight out without being questioned. It was still cool and she opted to walk for once rather than take the car. Suddenly she was reluctant to accept anything belonging to the Varonnes. She had surrendered her right to be one of them, and there was no place for her here now.

The village was already busy. In one of the streets adjoining the square a vegetable market was in full swing. At another time she would have enjoyed mingling, perhaps buying and eating, as she walked, some of the delicious fruit on display. But she was in a hurry. The nearer she got the quicker she walked. She could hardly wait to see him again, to see the possessive look that came into his eyes when they alighted on her.

Francois Montcalm was just coming out of the hotel as she approached it. Francesca had the feeling he might not have stopped to speak to her, only she gave him a hesitant smile.

'*Bonjour*, Madame Varonne,' he said in his solemn way.

'Good morning,' she beamed.

'Did you enjoy Ceyranne yesterday?'

The memory of it was still fresh in her mind and she knew a faint blush was staining her cheeks. 'Very much indeed.' She glanced past him, into the dim interior of the hotel. Would love always be this impatient? 'Is Mr. Devlin in?'

Francois Montcalm's face fell expressively. 'Alas, *madame*, he is out. He was just leaving when I came down to breakfast.' He bowed a little stiffly. '*Au revoir, madame.*'

'*Au revoir*,' she murmured.

She had so much wanted to see him. To hear his voice, be reassured by his common sense.

Francesca turned away from the hotel. How long would it be before she saw him again? Even half an hour would be too long.

She sank down into a chair by one of the tables. Disappointment plucked at her like angry hands. When the waiter appeared she ordered *café au lait* almost unthinkingly and silently admonished herself for behaving like an adolescent. Peter would not want her to pursue him relentlessly, to pine when he was out of her sight for a few hours.

When she had finished her coffee her disappointment was less intense, but she still had no desire to return to the château; to toil up the dusty road in the full glare of the sun to that cold, cheerless place which had been the Varonne family home for generations.

She wandered across to the shops at the far side of the square and slowly inspected the goods displayed in the windows. She had been absorbed by this occupation for several minutes when she had the weird feeling she was being watched.

Francesca twisted round sharply on her heel; her fierce expression gave way immediately to a smile at the sight of the small child who was watching her, his head slightly to one side. He was a beautiful child, about four years old with a mass of dark curly hair and a pair of eyes so dark that they were almost black.

'Hello,' she said, and realised immediately that a child of this age would not understand even so universal a greeting.

But to her surprise he answered ''Ello.'

She laughed and he laughed, and handed her his balloon on a stick.

Francesca took it from his plump, brown hand and admired it.

'*C'est joli,*' she said.

'You English?' he said, laughing again and pointing one fat finger at her.

'Do you speak English?' He nodded. 'What is your name?'

'Gilles.'

'And who taught you your English?'

'Papa.'

'Gilles!'

Both Francesca and the child looked startled. A plump woman, middle-aged and wearing unrelieved black was waving at him impatiently.

Francesca handed back the balloon. 'You'd better go, Gilles. Maman is calling.'

'Maman at home.'

He grinned engagingly again as he reached for the balloon. '*Au revoir, jolie madame,*' he said and as she looked down at such an enchanting child her heart gave a lurch of dismay and her smile faded. She put out her hand to detain him . . .

'Gilles!'

The child gave Francesca another smile and ran off to the woman who began to scold him noisily.

As he ran at the woman's side, his balloon held proudly aloft, Francesca could not draw her gaze away. She had seen those eyes before; the cast of the head was unmistakable. The child was without doubt a Varonne.

Drawing herself out of her shocked stupor, she started after them shouting, 'Madame, madame, wait!'

But they were too far away. Only Gilles's blue balloon was visible, like a beacon to guide her. They turned a corner and Francesca, who was panting breathlessly, ran into the narrow, cobbled street. She was just in time to see the woman and the child disappear into one of the houses.

Francesca ran, panting, up the street. She stepped back to make sure she hadn't made a mistake. She was sure it was this little house.

She knocked on the door, several

times, and stood back to gaze up at it impatiently. Every window was shuttered. She had almost come to the conclusion that she had been mistaken when the door opened a crack.

Francesca had expected to see the old woman so the sight of the young, pale face pressed to the crack was more than a surprise.

'Eloise!' she gasped. 'Do you live here?'

The door opened a fraction more, but not enough for Francesca to see inside. 'Yes, *madame*,' the girl said in a dull voice.

'Did a child come into this house?'

'Yes, *madame*.'

Francesca drew herself up from the wilting position that had become something of a habit to adopt and took a deep breath. It was all suddenly abundantly clear.

'He's yours?'

'Yes, *madame*.'

Eloise spoke in the same respectful monotone that was beginning to irritate Francesca. 'Where is his father?' she asked in a cold voice she hardly recognised as her own.

Eloise's gaze did not leave Francesca's face. 'Gilles has no father, *madame*.'

Eloise was about to close the door when Francesca put out a hand to stop her. 'Just one moment,' she said in an authoritative voice that succeeded in stopping Eloise from closing the door in her face. 'I know that Paul is his father, but I want you to know I'm not angry, nor do I wish to take Gilles away from you, and I don't want to make any trouble for you. But I do want to be sure he has everything he needs. Has he been provided for? Do you have everything you need?'

For the first time the girl's lips curved into a smile. 'We are well-cared for, *madame*. The Varonnes look after their own. Thank you for your concern, but there is nothing you can do to help.'

The door closed at last and Francesca knew she could do no more. Slowly she walked down the street towards the centre of the village. The need for Peter was even more acute. The shock of realising the child was Paul's was only just beginning to affect her, and she began to tremble.

As she walked backwards down the street she never took her eyes from that neat little house and its firmly closed door. Then she began to run as fast as she could until she reached the street market where she had to slow down in order to push her way blindly towards the square. She was quite unaware of the hostile stares she was attracting, and the muttered complaints about her rudeness.

When she had told Peter she knew Paul had been unfaithful, the knowledge had come from some inner source. Now that she had seen the evidence with her own eyes she was shattered. How many more had there been? Chantal? Her knowing look. *Paul and I were very close . . .*

Francesca's mind returned to all those parties. To the proprietorial way so many women spoke to him. Jane

Hervey, the wife of one of Paul's directors. She was blonde and brassy and condescendingly kind to Francesca, pitying almost. And Jane Hervey had been heartbroken when Paul died.

How many more?

How can a woman live with a man for five years and not know him? she thought frantically.

How different was her relationship with Peter. They'd met only days ago and yet already she was sure she knew him better than she ever knew Paul. He was undoubtedly a man with high principles, someone she could trust, and she badly needed to see him now.

She was even more breathless when she ran into the hotel. Madame Oisin was behind the desk and Francesca realised that she must look rather wild. Automatically she made a frantic attempt to smooth her hair and appear more composed than she really was, than she possibly could be.

'*Je suis Madame Varonne . . .* ' she gasped.

'Yes, *madame*, I know; you are from the château. Can I help you?' the woman asked in careful English.

Francesca was relieved that having to make herself understood by this woman was not going to be added to the day's tribulations. 'I'm looking for Mr. Devlin. Is he in?'

The woman glanced at the keyboard behind the desk and shook her head. 'Mr. Devlin is still out. He went out early this morning with three men who called to see him.'

'What men?' asked Francesca in amazement.

Madame Oisin shrugged. 'I do not know. I have never seen them before. Can I give the monsieur a message when he returns?'

'Yes, yes please,' Francesca answered eagerly. 'Tell him I want to see him as soon as possible. You mustn't forget. It's very important that I see him as soon as he comes in.'

The woman nodded and eyed Francesca curiously. 'I will not forget, *madame*;

please be assured. Can I do anything else for you?'

Francesca looked at her blankly. Why, oh why wasn't Peter here when she needed him so?

'*Madame*, is there anything more you require?'

'Yes, yes there is,' she answered, making a conscious effort to appear normal. 'I'm told your husband has the only taxi in St. Marcel. I don't fancy walking all the way back up the hill. Is he free?'

'Certainly he is.' She banged her fist down on the desk bell. 'Pasquale will take you back to the château and I will give Mr. Devlin your message.'

Francesca was paying Pasquale when Julien came round the side of the château from the direction of the garage.

He looked startled for the moment and then a broad smile appeared on his face. It suddenly occurred to Francesca that her initial dislike of him was entirely due to his resemblance to Paul.

'Francesca, why did you not take the car?' he asked, as the taxi drew away.

'I wanted a walk, but I couldn't face coming back up the hill.'

His face broke into a smile. 'That is always the disadvantage. Chantal, she always walks down but always she persuades someone to bring her back.'

He gave a little laugh. What a family, thought Francesca. Chantal, the daughter of a gypsy, who bore the name of Varonne, and Paul's son living in the village with no right to the name at all. Suddenly Francesca felt very tired. The sooner she severed her ties with these people the better she would feel.

'May I speak to you in private, Julien?'

The smile left his face. 'Berthe told me about Mr. Devlin. I hope you are certain of what you are doing, Francesca. It is very soon. Personally, I had not expected it of you, to forget Paul so quickly.'

'I assure you, Julien, I have not forgotten Paul, but I don't wish to speak to you about that. I have no intention of discussing my relationship with Peter with you, because I couldn't hope to make you understand. This matter is something quite different.'

He frowned and stood aside for her to pass. 'Of course. We will go into the library. There we will not be disturbed.'

The library was the one room on the ground floor that was in use. The room smelled slightly musty and the books that lined its walls looked as if they'd been undisturbed for years.

Julien took some papers off a chair but she said quickly, 'I don't want to sit down. What I have to say will take only a minute.' Julien straightened up and looked at her questioningly. Francesca took a deep breath. 'That girl — Eloise. The one we saw when we went to the vineyard . . . '

Julien turned away and began to tidy some papers on his desk. 'Yes, Eloise . . . ?'

'I saw her today, and the child.'

The papers slipped out of his hand and his lips tightened into an angry line. He thumped his fist on the desk.

'She told you! She had no right! She was warned no one was to know . . . '

'No, Julien, she did not tell me, but I do have eyes in my head and that child is Paul's.'

Julien relaxed slightly and gave her an apologetic smile. 'I am sorry that you had to know.'

'Well, it might have had the power to hurt me once upon a time. That child is no more than four so it seems obvious the affair was going on very shortly after our marriage, if not before. I remember he did come here several times in the months following the wedding.' She gave a bitter little laugh. 'I missed him,' she added softly. More briskly she went on, 'All I feel now, Julien, is anger because I've been treated like an idiot. I've no intention of causing an hysterical scene, anyway, so have no fear, but I am anxious to know what is being done for the boy. Eloise said they were being looked after, but knowing these people and their pride, I'd like to be sure. If not I intend to make ample provision for him myself. Paul left me more money than I'd ever need even if I weren't contemplating getting married again.'

Julien sat down behind the desk and spread his hands on its leather top. 'You need not trouble. The cottage is part of the Varonne estate, so their home will always be secure. Eloise's brother, as you have already been told, is studying in Paris at the Sorbonne.' He eyed Francesca steadily. 'I've no need to tell you that without our help such an education would be impossible for him.

'As for the child himself, he is looked after by Eloise and, when she is not there, by his grandmother. When he is old enough he will be sent to one of the best schools in France. The arrangements have already been made.'

Francesca nodded. 'That's all I wanted to know, Julien. Thank you.'

She was about to go but she hesitated a moment and then asked harshly, 'Are there any more?'

Julien looked at her sharply and she

added, 'Of Paul's, I mean.'

He looked shocked. 'No, of course not. It was only a foolish youthful escapade.'

'He is still Paul's son. Why don't you make him the official heir to Varonne?'

He looked even more shocked now as he groped for an answer. 'I couldn't possibly do that. Marguerite . . . '

'Marguerite will never know. She's unlikely to outlive you, Julien.'

'That is in doubt. Her family are a long-lived one. In any case . . . '

'It was only a suggestion. I didn't expect you to act on it.'

Julien jumped to his feet as she started towards the door. He looked relieved. 'I must say you are taking this in an admirable fashion, Francesca.'

She stopped. 'Didn't you?' He looked away and she smiled tightly. 'There is little that has the power to shock me any more, Julien.'

She went back up the stairs feeling numb now that the interview with Julien was over. As she reached the upper landing an icy blast of wind tugged at her skirt and ruffled her hair, causing her flesh to goosepimple. When she turned the corner she was just in time to see the door closing.

Francesca walked the full length of the corridor. Ninon was sitting by the closed door. Automatically Francesca picked the cat up and tucked it under her arm, walking slowly back to her room.

Inside she glanced round, vaguely, like one in a daze, aware that weeks, no days, ago, what had happened that morning would have devastated her.

Ninon squirmed in her tight grip and automatically Francesca let her go. Immediately the cat ran to the door and began to scratch at it.

Francesca watched her without really seeing. The air was filled with the unmistakable aroma of *Hombre*.

She rushed across to the window and opened it as wide as it would go, then she turned back, scanning every corner of the room. The feeling that someone had been there recently was so strong it was almost tangible.

Someone had been in her room. She touched the things lying on her dressing-table, frantically trying to remember how she had left them. It was impossible.

She stood with her back to the dressing-table, breathing heavily, fighting back panic. The horrible feeling of being watched was starting again and she dreaded it as much as the physical symptoms of some fatal disease.

The curtain flapped in the breeze and brushed against her cheek. She flinched away from it, choking back a sob. She closed her eyes and forced herself to be calm again. When she opened her eyes again the panic had gone.

Her eyes when she opened them focused at last on Ninon who was still scratching at the door. Ninon.

Francesca could see Paul quite clearly, sitting in his favourite chair in the flat, swinging from side to side, a glass of brandy balanced in one hand.

'That cat,' he would say with a laugh,

'she follows me everywhere. Do you know, Fran, she won't let me go out alone even in the car! Every time, she manages to get out and jumps into the car with me. And there she stays! Wherever I go she's with me in the passenger seat. She's almost human that cat.'

And Paul's car had dived off a cliff.

Francesca couldn't tear her eyes from the cat. 'You tried to tell me, didn't you, Ninon? All this time you tried so hard to tell me.'

She walked over to the door and opened it. Ninon shot out of the room and along the corridor. Francesca followed. She followed her along the corridor and out of the door. Ninon streaked up the steps and Francesca followed.

The door to the tower room was ajar and Francesca walked right in. This time she felt none of the dread her previous visit had caused.

He was standing by the window. He had changed quite a lot. His hair was longer and he was much thinner. His face had lost the roundness that endless brandies and expense account luncheons had given it. And he wore a beard.

'Hello, Paul,' she said and her voice seemed to come from far away.

'Hello, Franny. I wondered when you would come.'

'I'd have come earlier, only I was always a little stupid. It took me a long time to realise.'

'Don't feel bad about it. It wasn't intended that you should — yet.'

She looked around her, yet saw nothing. 'Why, Paul? In God's name, why?'

'That isn't an easy question to answer in a few words. Sit down, Fran. We have time, and six months to make up for.'

Automatically she sank down onto the divan, next to Ninon who was licking her paws unconcernedly. 'You have much more than six months to make up for, Paul,' she said in a bitter voice she could hardly recognise as her own. 'Why didn't you let me know you were alive? Why didn't you let me know the day you came from the west wing? I nearly died of fright. And the night I visited your mother. You were in the room then, but you didn't let me know. You actually hid from me.'

'I had to,' he answered apologetically. 'I really couldn't tell you just yet. It was for your own protection.'

'They all knew, didn't they?' She laughed brokenly. 'Poor Marguerite and her hallucinations! They all knew. Chantal was laughing at me all the time. All of them knew but me.'

'I wouldn't let them tell you. Maman doesn't know anything anyway. She just thinks we've come here to live at last.'

'I suppose you were responsible for telling her I had a miscarriage.'

'I could hardly tell her you were grief-stricken over my death,' he answered wryly.

She looked at him again. 'Why? Are you going to tell me why you did this unspeakable thing?'

He took a bottle and two glasses from the bottom of the wardrobe. 'Have a drink, Fran.'

She shook her head. 'No thanks. I want nothing from you but an explanation. You had no insurance so it couldn't have been for that.'

His calm, her own calm, amazed her. It was as if nothing had ever happened.

'And why did you let them send for me now? Why now, Paul?'

'Simple,' he answered, smiling in the urbane way she knew so well. 'It was the right time. You couldn't come before because you were ill. We couldn't cope with you while you were having a mental breakdown. I got Berthe to send for you as soon as you were able to come.'

She watched him as he filled his glass to the rim. 'I suppose I should feel grateful for that.'

He sat back in his chair and regarded her sombrely for a moment or two. 'You look good, Fran. Really good. You've lost some weight but that can soon be remedied. You've always looked good. Innocent and untouched.'

She hated his use of her name. How different it was to Peter's gentle 'Francesca.' Peter. Oh, heavens, she thought, biting her lip. Peter.

'You don't look exactly overjoyed at seeing me, darling. It's quite unlike my Fran.'

She shivered. 'I was just congratulating myself on not being carried away screaming. In the circumstances you must agree I'd be entitled to.' He laughed. 'Oh,' she added in a strangely conversational tone, 'I saw your son this morning. Congratulations. He looks very much like you. It's very probable he'll grow up into a charmer too.'

His laughter ended abruptly. 'Gilles.'

'Yes, Gilles. Your image. Eloise's son.'

He buried his face in the glass. 'It was nothing, Fran. It was over years ago.'

'Nothing.' At last she began to feel something — anger. 'You were having an affair literally during our honeymoon and you ask me to believe it was nothing. And I know you were there this morning. Eloise was scared stiff I'd go in.'

'Lately I've taken foolish chances because I just couldn't stand being cooped up here any longer. I knew someone was at the door but she didn't say who it was though.'

'Nothing,' she scoffed as if he hadn't spoken. 'You've carried on an affair that's lasted as long as our marriage — and for all I know it may have been longer — and you say it's nothing. Please, Paul, don't take me for a fool any longer.

'I was a child while I was married to you, a mindless child at that. I was like an obedient pet to you, petted and patronised. But please believe I've begun to think for myself. The thinking process started the day you died and because it developed late, and because I've come to enjoy thinking for myself, it isn't easy to turn off again.

'Is Eloise the reason you did your disappearing trick? If she is she can have you. Don't think I would stand in your way.'

He laughed again. 'Good grief, no, Fran. You can believe what you like, but Eloise isn't important to me.'

'Or Chantal?'

'Chantal can be very persistent, and I've been lonely. As I said, life hasn't been very easy for me here and Chantal has been a great help to me.'

'I bet!'

'Why won't you believe me when I say I missed you, Fran?'

She looked away from him. 'You make me sick.'

'I had to go, Fran. Believe me. I had to go and quickly. If there had been any other course open to me I would have taken it. Do you think I enjoy being incarcerated in this place for weeks on end? Don't you know me better than that?'

'What trouble were you in, Paul? Was it trouble with your job? Were you . . . ?'

'Was I embezzling?' He laughed. 'I was never near enough to the money to have a chance.' He refilled his glass. 'It was something far bigger than that, Fran. You'd better sit back.'

'You couldn't have committed any crime, Paul, or I'd have known about it.'

He smiled to himself. 'Does the name Domenic mean anything to you?'

She frowned. 'Domenic,' she repeated. 'Yes, it is familiar.'

'It should be. Think about it.'

He sat there, totally at ease, cradling the brandy in one hand and smiling at her. Oh, how he is enjoying himself, she thought.

Suddenly she remembered where she had heard the name before. The case had filled the headlines; Domenic was the name on the lips of every newscaster on the television and the radio. It had happened just after she'd had the news of Paul's accident and nothing seemed important then.

'Geoffrey Domenic,' she said. 'He was the scientist who was arrested for spying. He had been giving away priceless information over a number of years, along with some other people who were unrelated to him, also in top secret jobs. They were all arrested at about the same time and the trial was sensational. Domenic had done it because he was being blackmailed over some currency deals he'd been involved in during the war and was never found out.'

'You're very well-informed Francesca. I never thought you were so interested in current affairs.'

'There's very little else to do in a nursing home but read newspapers. They have the peculiarity of being a link with normality. You have no idea how comforting it is to know people are still murdering, raping and thieving when you're incarcerated in one of those places.'

His eyes narrowed. 'They treated you well?'

'Couldn't have been better. It didn't even look like a lunatic asylum, except for the bars at the windows.' Her voice hardened. 'We were talking about Geoffrey Domenic.'

'Yes, so we were,' he said with a sigh. 'Well, the papers may have had a gala day with the case, but there was a lot they missed out too. A lot they had to miss out. They caught Domenic and those other poor devils who had been selling secrets, but they didn't get the missing Mr. X, as he was referred to during the trial, who was doing the blackmailing and collecting the infor- mation. There was nothing said because he eluded them. Me.'

She gaped at him. 'You must be joking, Paul.'

He smiled. 'One of the qualities I liked about you best was your unshake- able faith in me. It really started years before I met you, when I joined the Communist Party at University. It was my father's idea; he'd always been a sympathiser. It didn't mean much to me but I agreed. Things just went on from there. By the time I was given one of the most important jobs in England, politics were of no account. It was the excitement of being a totally unknown quantity to my family and closest friends. I was doing a job that was both important and dangerous, and I loved every minute of it — that and the money. My job was a perfect cover for my activities, of course. I travelled to and fro on legitimate business all the time. I never made a contact in the same place twice. I expect that's why I had a good long run.'

Francesca shook her head. 'You couldn't have done it without my knowing.'

'My dear Fran, if you'd have known I would have been no good for the job. The fact that even my own wife didn't know was proof of my success. I chose you for my wife because you were so delightfully innocent. I've always liked women, but I couldn't afford to get involved with someone who might be too curious about me. You had no family who might ask questions. You were so perfect you might have been made for me.'

'How romantic,' she said bitterly.

'Don't be like that, Fran. I made you happy. I was a good husband. You had no cause for complaint.'

'Well, I have now. I don't like the idea of being married to a blackmailer and a traitor.'

'That's just what I've been since you met me, Fran. I was no different on our wedding day. I don't regret one moment of it, and what is more, I've always been fond of you, Fran.'

She ignored him. 'How did you get away?'

He lit himself a cigarette without offering one to her. 'Domenic thought he was under suspicion and came crying to me. As it turned out he was right and for all I know he led them to me too. Or they might have known before. He was scared stiff and liable to panic. He didn't know my real name, but I had the feeling it would be better if I got out of the country for a while just to see what happened. I was, naturally, prepared for this eventuality. I had a false passport ready. It's amazing just what money can buy, Fran. That's how I got out. If I'd tried to leave with my own passport I doubt if I'd got as far as the airport. As it happened it wasn't a moment too soon. Domenic and the others were arrested the minute they realised I'd gone, which made me realise I'd been right about them suspecting me.'

'Why didn't you go behind the Iron Curtain? Isn't that what's usually done?'

'Because, as I said, politics don't interest me.' He was speaking to her in his more familiar patronising tone, explaining as if she were a child, 'And you know I like to enjoy myself. I earned a lot of money — a fortune. I want to be able to spend it in style. And this way I might be useful again. It's happened before. Another country, a new identity. A life of indefinite leisure isn't my ideal. Eventually I'll need the excitement again.'

'You can't do anything of that sort

while you're here, Paul.'

'No, I realise that. I don't suppose my 'death' will have fooled the experts for a moment, and they'll still be kicking themselves for letting me get away. That's why I sent for you.'

'Bait,' she whispered. 'To see if I would be followed.'

He leaned forward, eager to explain. 'It's like a game of cat and mouse, Fran, with each side waiting to make the move. Someone has to make the move or it will remain stalemate, and that won't do. I don't want to stay here for ever, however safe it may be.'

Her eyes flashed with hatred. 'You're abominable, Paul. I worshipped you. You were like a god to me. Now I can't even summon enough emotion to despise you.'

He smiled smugly. 'You'll get over it, my darling. You're shocked, which is natural. I'm still me, I haven't changed.'

'But I have.'

He studied her carefully for a moment. 'Yes, Franny,' he said slowly, 'I do believe that you have.'

She got to her feet and walked over to the window. 'What do you do next, Paul?' she asked in a voice that was still remarkably calm.

'That is the problem,' he admitted. 'I hadn't wanted you to see me just yet. It's too soon. Your coming here will undoubtedly be noted. The British secret service isn't so easily convinced by an accidental death at such a providential moment. Unfortunately it was something of a panic move.

'I suppose the best plan is for you and me to go over the border into Spain and stay there for a while.' She looked at him in astonishment. 'I have all the documents,' he assured her. 'There's money in Madrid, South America and Switzerland. We're rich. We can live in great style, Fran. I was well-prepared. I even made sure you were well-provided for when I went, didn't I?'

'Just like you've provided for your son, and heaven knows how many other liabilities. You seem to think money is the answer to everything, Paul. It isn't. I'd prefer to have a husband I can respect and when Gilles is old enough to know, I'm certain he'll prefer a father he can look up to.'

She shuddered. 'Well, I don't want any part of that money, Paul. I'd rather starve than live on any money of yours.'

He came across to her and gripped her shoulders. 'But you have done — all these years. I've had to be careful, admittedly, but we still lived well because I knew I had all that security behind me, just waiting to be spent. Even that nice expensive nursing home was paid for out of my ill-gotten gains. Has that fact escaped you?'

She twisted round. 'The nursing home!' she gasped. 'All those people I thought were watching me.' She buried her head in her hands, laughing hysterically. 'They were real! Oh, heavens. I was being followed, watched, and the flat *was* searched.'

'I expect so. They wouldn't question you. You'd either be lying your head off or you'd actually know nothing. Either way a dead end for them. They knew if I was alive you were the only link. That's why I had you come now — to convince them I was dead.'

She stopped laughing and looked at him. Sheer animal ferocity contorted her face. 'Do you know what you've done? What I went through? Have you any notion at all? I thought I was going insane! All our so-called friends turned away from me. I was totally alone, and it was your fault. You did that to me, Paul. You put me into that black, endless limbo!'

She began to pound at him, but he caught her by the wrists. His face twisted viciously as he forced her hands down and she began to cry uncontrollably. 'Stop it, Fran! It wasn't my fault. You were innocent. There was no danger to you. How was I to know you'd crack up? How were they to know you'd actually notice being watched and followed?

'How would you have liked being the

wife of a convicted spy? Think of that. There'd be journalists at your door, photographers wherever you went, and me in jail for forty years. Would you have preferred to go insane that way, Fran?'

He let her go and gave her his handkerchief. She sank down onto the divan again, all passion spent.

'Have you ever thought of anyone other than yourself?'

'Listen to me, Fran, and listen very carefully. We're leaving for Spain together today. We'll get a villa on the coast and stay for a while. We can even raise a family. You've always wanted children.'

'I never said so,' she murmured, twisting the handkerchief in her hands.

'No, because you were always afraid of speaking up to me, afraid of displeasing me in any way.'

She took a deep breath and looked at him at last. 'It's too late, Paul. Much too late. Six months of believing you dead can't be forgotten, and I hate what you are.'

'You're giving way to emotion, Fran. I've already told you, I'm still the same man you married.'

'The difference is, Paul, I'm not the same woman you married. What has happened has changed me. Besides, hasn't Berthe or Chantal told you? I've fallen in love with someone else, and it's different. I'm not an adolescent any more. I love him as a woman, Paul. I love him as I never loved you.'

The harshness of his laughter made her flinch. 'You are still an adolescent, Fran. Who do you think he is? Oh, I do know all about it. I've known all about him since the day you both arrived. He's used you, and he's used Chantal. He's used you both to get at me. A chance meeting in Bordeaux!' he scoffed. 'Now you know why I've had to stay in hiding since you came, why I couldn't let you know I was alive. He's the one they sent after me!'

She stared at him. 'Oh no. No, you're wrong. He's just a civil servant.'

'Another name for someone who

works for the government,' supplied Paul, laughing again. 'And I can tell you he's not alone. The others aren't far away.'

Francois Montcalm, she thought, and the three men who had been there when he hadn't expected to see her.

He had always been available, waiting to see her, asking questions. Innocent questions. He was so interested in the château, its rooms. Chantal had known. How she must have enjoyed her knowledge. And Peter? The pain was almost too much for her to bear. The memory of his treacherous kisses would haunt her for ever. She could have been so happy with him. Now there was nothing.

She buried her head in her hands. 'I can't bear it.'

'You'll have to, Fran. He's used you. He's quite good at asking questions, but he's learned nothing because Chantal's clever, and you knew nothing. By making up to you he's tried to draw me out. What man would knowingly sit back and allow his wife to be made love to by another man? It's all very simple, isn't it, darling?'

'Stop it, please, Paul!'

'Well, be sensible, dear. Grow up.'

'You sent me out there to him. No wonder they were suddenly so eager to lend me a car. You knew he'd be waiting.'

'He was making no move to go so I had to do something. You were ideally suited to him, easily convinced. You must have been the answer to his prayers, Fran, and to mine, come to think of it. Your act was too good to be false.'

'I trusted him.'

'Let it be a lesson to you — trust no one. He's not for you, Fran. You probably won't cause him a moment's thought when this is over. I'm his objective. Perhaps your willingness to fall into his arms might have allayed his suspicions a little, which is all to the good. I'm sure you talked very convincingly about my death. Chantal did, I know that. They'll have spoken to your doctor too. No faking the reason for your nervous breakdown. It couldn't have been better if we'd planned it. Yes, it's very possible that you convinced them I really did kill myself in my haste to get away,' he went on thoughtfully and then, glancing at her, 'You'd better tell me everything you know, Fran. I need the information.'

She flashed him a venomous look. 'Do you really think Chantal could have fooled him, if he's the man you say?'

'No, I dare say he wasn't fooled, but Chantal has been with him a great deal of the time and so have you. He's been kept away from the château, and that's the important thing. He's learned nothing to make him believe I'm alive.'

He came up to her. It nauseated her to think she had loved this man for five long years.

'Now, are you going to answer my questions?' She said nothing. 'You know something, Fran?' he said in a conversational tone. 'You can't exist without a man to look after you, and I'm the only one you have left now.' She stared at him and he said patiently, 'I shouldn't bother to protect him, if I were you, Fran. Remember who he is and who I am.'

'I'm never likely to forget. What is it you want to know?'

He smiled. 'Did anyone question you after I left?' She shook her head. 'No, I assumed they wouldn't. They stood to learn more by watching and waiting.' She shivered. 'Has Devlin anyone with him?' She didn't answer. 'Fran?'

His voice was hard. She put her hand to her head, closed her eyes in an attempt to clear her mind of the one fact that was hammering at her brain — Peter had betrayed her.

'There's a Frenchman staying at the hotel,' she answered in a dull voice. 'Francois Montcalm. I saw him at Bordeaux too.'

'Yes, the French will be in this one too,' he murmured, thoughtfully nibbling at his thumbnail. 'Anyone else?' he shot at her.

'When I went to see him this

morning Madame Oisin said he was out
— with three men.'

For a moment Paul said nothing and
then, thoughtfully again, 'We'd best
leave straight away. There's no point in
my taking more chances. Once away
from here there's no chance of them
catching me.' He looked at her, 'I have
more money put away than you'd ever
believe!'

'Even if you were diamond-studded,
Paul, I couldn't live with you again,' she
said in a cold, clear voice. She clasped
her hands composedly in her lap.

'I'll do anything you ask but I won't
come with you.'

He sat next to her on the bed and put
his arms around her shoulders. She
stiffened beneath his touch. 'Hasn't the
fact that he doesn't really want you,
sunk in yet?'

She closed her eyes in a useless
attempt to alleviate the pain of that
knowledge. 'I realise it well enough,
Paul. I was a fool. I've always been a
fool. But I still don't want to come with

you. I can't bear you, and I won't live the life of a fugitive just to pander to your sense of excitement. You can't even pretend to love me.'

'I can't let you go,' he said softly.

'Kill me then. My life means nothing to me now.'

He laughed. 'Don't be so melodramatic. I'm not a killer. I couldn't harm anyone, much less you, but I can't let you go. You'd fall for someone else's charms in no time, and then what would you do? Marry him? You'd want a divorce first. Can't you see how impossible it would be?'

She shrugged away from him. 'I've loved you and I've loved Peter. After that how could I fall in love again?' She turned to look at him. 'What you said before, about Peter following me here to get to you . . . well, then, they're just waiting for you to leave with me. If you go alone and I'm seen to stay, no one will know you've gone. They really will believe you're dead then. I'll go back to England and you'll be free.'

'No, Fran,' he said, shaking his head. 'I'm not letting you go. You'd tell him. Oh, I know you wouldn't mean to, but you'd tell him. He'd know you'd seen me. Besides,' he added softly, 'over the years we've been together I've grown fond of you, and now you've changed — for the better. You've got more fire now. I find that very attractive.'

She jumped to her feet and he said, 'What choice have you, Fran? A life in a flat on your own. No friends, suspicious of anyone you meet? Or a life of luxury with me?' She said nothing. 'Damn it, Francesca! You're still my wife. You owe me some loyalty. I need you to get me out of here.'

There was a fractional silence and then she said, 'All right, Paul, I'll come. As you say there's nothing else for me. What do you want me to do?'

'Drive out of here with me hidden in the back of the car.'

Her mind was so numb with misery that she couldn't even feel disgust any more. 'The sooner the better,' she said,

286

moving towards the door.

As she passed him he caught hold of her and pressed his lips against her neck. 'I'll make it up to you, Fran. You see if I don't. Don't pine for this other fellow. You don't really care for him. You can't after what we meant to each other.'

'I'll come with you,' she repeated, pulling away from him, 'but don't you dare to touch me, Paul, ever again.'

His hands dropped to his side as he stared at her in astonishment. After it all, she marvelled, he could still be surprised.

Before she could move right away from him the door opened and Chantal came rushing in. She stopped abruptly at the sight of Francesca and then she said, 'What are you doing here?'

'Speaking to my husband.'

'What are you going to do?'

'She's going to be a good and dutiful wife and get me out of here,' answered Paul.

Chantal's eyes opened wide and she

shook her head in disbelief. 'Oh no, Paul. No, you promised.' She rushed across the room and pressed herself into his arms. 'I won't let you go. After all your promises to me, I can't let you go.'

He held her close and there was nothing but amusement in his eyes. 'Now, don't be a silly child. You know Francesca is my wife.'

Chantal sobbed heartbrokenly. 'I was the one who helped you all these months. All she has done is take on your enemy as a lover. I'll do anything you ask, Paul, only don't leave me.' She turned on Francesca. 'How can you go with him? He even thought it was fun coming to my room because it was next to yours. He enjoyed that!'

Francesca turned away. 'I'll go and pack my things.'

'I won't let Paul go,' she screamed after her, and then, 'You promised we'd always be together, Paul. I won't let her have you!'

Francesca walked slowly down the

stairs with Chantal's screams and curses echoing in her ears. When she had reached the half landing she closed the door thankfully behind her, but Chantal's voice could still be heard.

10

Afterwards Francesca was to be grateful for the total numbness that had taken over her emotions during her meeting with Paul. Mercifully she was unable to feel anything. The desolation would come later, but now she was able to go about the practical business of packing her clothes with a body and mind anaesthetised to all pain.

She had just finished packing when the door opened. She turned her unseeing eyes from the view from her window, expecting that Paul had come for her, but it was Chantal. Her face was swollen and her eyes red from all the tears she had shed, and there were two black streaks down her face where she had brushed them away. Somewhere deep inside her, Francesca felt a stirring of pity.

'Where's Paul?' Francesca asked.

'Saying goodbye to Marguerite. He is telling her he is taking you for a long holiday. Aunt Marguerite agrees it would be good for you.'

'I'm sorry, Chantal. I really am.'

'Aunt Marguerite used to hate you. She never forgave Paul for marrying a nobody. Paul promised to divorce you; he knew, you see, she would accept you then. Marguerite does not believe in divorce. Better that Paul's son should have the blood of a nobody than the blood of a gypsy like me. Better that there should be no son at all and the family name not soiled by divorce.'

'There'll be no more legitimate Varonnes,' said Francesca. 'It's time the Varonnes ceased to stain the human racc.'

'You don't love him.'

'No.'

Chantal came right into the room and then gazed around her, turning back to Francesca. 'You love Peter Devlin?'

'Yes. That makes two fools — you and me.'

'I love Paul. I love him more than you could ever love Peter Devlin. I've loved Paul ever since I can remember. Now you are taking him away and I hate you because I shall never see him again.'

'Perhaps it's as well. You're very young. Paul cares for no one. He brings only misery to those who come into contact with him.'

'Paul is bad. I have always known it, but it makes no difference to me.'

Paul appeared in the doorway. He glanced anxiously at them both and said tersely, 'Are you ready, Fran?'

She nodded and he took her case from the bed. Chantal looked away. He kissed her lightly on the cheek but she still did not look up.

When Berthe appeared in the doorway she flashed a strained smile at Francesca and said, 'Come, Chantal, we shall watch from the tower.'

'No, Maman,' she answered in a dull voice, 'I will not watch at all.'

She followed her mother from the room and just as she reached the door she turned, her eyes brimming with tears. '*Au revoir*, Chantal,' said Paul.

'Goodbye, Paul,' she answered.

When they had gone he looked at Francesca and smiled confidently. His clothes were casual and as immaculate as ever. He looked as if he were going on holiday.

'We can get to the garage through the kitchen. We'd best go that way. As you've probably realised. Madame Resaque and Jeanne are completely trustworthy.'

'Haven't you realised that Peter will wonder where I've gone?'

'Berthe will tell him you've changed your mind — for the moment anyway. She'll tell him you've gone away for a while to think it over.'

'He'll never believe that.'

He shrugged. 'He can't prove anything else.'

'Poor Chantal,' Francesca said a moment later, smiling bitterly. 'She believes every word you said.'

'I never promised her anything,' he

answered, ushering her quickly along the corridor that led to the kitchen. 'It isn't my fault she attached more importance to our relationship than I intended. We did spend a great deal of time together at first. I couldn't leave the tower with all the people calling to pay their respects after the accident; and, for all I knew, there were government agents amongst them. It was hell, trying to keep Maman away. She had to be drugged, of course. Luckily everyone understood the need for that. Chantal was company for me. I even taught her a trick or two in case of need; in case anyone should come and ask *too* many awkward questions.'

'What tricks?'

'There are tricks Chantal knows that no one has to teach her. She can bedevil a man just by looking at him.'

'Yes, I know about that,' she said sharply. 'What other tricks?'

'I taught her how to cut through the brake cable of a car, in case I was in danger of arrest, so that there would be an unfortunate accident. I reckoned that if anyone came snooping round and became too suspicious, he would have to go away again for orders and reinforcements. This would make sure he'd never get there.'

She stopped as they came to the kitchen door. 'You'd actually do that?'

He looked abashed. '*I* couldn't; I admit it. I wouldn't have the guts. Chantal, though, would do anything, especially for me. Just anything.'

Francesca smiled grimly. 'You have the uncanny talent for using everyone in accordance to their talents. My stupidity, Chantal's lack of scruples . . . '

'You don't seem to realise it's them or me.'

'Would you have told her to tamper with Peter's car?'

'If he'd become too suspicious. It wasn't something I wanted to do, but your boy-friend would have had no compunction about killing me rather than letting me escape.'

He pushed open the kitchen door.

He even paused for a word with Madame Resaque and Jeanne who were busily preparing the dinner. Francesca was not even aware of missing lunch.

They crossed the narrow courtyard to the garage. 'We're taking the Fiat,' he said as he opened the boot and flung in the cases. 'It's less spectacular.'

Francesca watched him. Was it only twenty-four hours since Peter had held her in his arms and promised her the world? Or was it another age, another time?

'What if I see Peter in the village?' she asked.

Paul shrugged. 'Smile and wave, but don't stop. Make out that you're on an errand for Berthe.'

Francesca saw this as the pattern of her life in the future; playing a part, always pretending. Living with Paul when she loathed him. Living without Peter. Above all living without Peter.

Suddenly she slumped against the car. 'I can't do it, Paul,' she said in a shaky voice. 'I just can't. I'm sorry.

You'll have to go without me.'

He gripped her shoulder so hard that she winced. 'You'll have to. Don't be so bloody simple for once. How on earth do you think I'd get through the village if I were behind the wheel?

'I can't do it myself, Francesca, but I'm going. If they catch me you'll have that on your conscience. I can't stand it here any longer. It's been pure agony cooped up in the château, big as it is, all these months. That's why I'm taking this chance on leaving now. I wouldn't last five minutes in jail.'

She straightened up. 'In the past few months I've done my share of feeling sorry for myself but now I feel sorry for you, Paul. You're pathetic.'

He released her abruptly. 'You don't need to feel sorry for me. Now let's move. If we're caught now you're for it too, you know. No one will possibly believe you didn't know I was alive all these months.'

'Get in, Paul,' she told him coldly. Her lips curled into a mirthless smile. 'I couldn't desert such a pathetic creature as you. You said before I couldn't live without a man to care for me; well, that isn't quite the truth. It's you who needs to be cared for all the time. Me, Chantal, poor Eloise; even Jane Hervey.'

He looked startled, but she held up the rug for him to get under and a moment later they were on their way. Francesca gave all her concentration to the driving in an effort to stop herself thinking. As the road twisted downwards the car gathered momentum and she let it go faster, feeling reckless, not caring if the car took the corners fast and too sharply.

'Slow down,' said Paul from the back. 'We don't want to look as if we're running. Slow down, you idiot.'

Obediently Francesca put her foot on the brake but the car sped onwards regardless. 'Paul!' she cried in panic, 'It doesn't work!'

She pressed her foot down again and again. He clambered over the seat to sit beside her. 'Try the gears.'

'They're jammed!'

'God in heaven, how did this happen?'

'It's no use praying to a God you don't believe in, Paul.' Suddenly she began to laugh. 'Chantal! She knew about this when she said she'd never see you again. You taught her well, Paul!'

His foot was crushing hers, pushing the brake down to the floor, but the car sped on, crazily down the hill. She cried out in pain as his foot clamped down on hers, but the cry was lost in the wind. The pain shot up her leg and she screamed again and again.

Paul pulled at the handbrake but the car was already out of control, and then he jerked her away from the wheel and she fell back against the seat. The car careered off the road into the terraced vineyard and they were thrown crazily back and forth as it tore through the vines for what seemed like an endless time. It was only seconds. The car was slowed by the growing vines but the vineyard was only a narrow strip of land and the edge of the hill came relentlessly closer. Paul wrenched the wheel sideways again and automatically Francesca covered her face with her arms as a tree loomed ahead. Then the world turned upside down. Francesca heard a scream that might have been her own, a splintering of glass and a deafening crash of metal. Then the nightmare ended in dreamless sleep.

* * *

'She is coming round now, monsieur.'

Francesca opened her eyes and saw only half of the man within her line of vision, like a dummy in a store window. She could smell burning leaves. It was the smell of autumn, only this was June. Her father had always burned leaves in autumn and she always helped him to collect them. She had missed that after he died.

She opened her eyes again and could see all of Peter clearly, so she judged he was crouched down beside her. He gave her the funny lopsided grin and it was as if the last few hours had never been.

'I hate you,' she said, recollecting everything almost immediately.

'Hate me all you want, darling, only please don't move. A doctor and an ambulance are on their way, and until the doctor's seen you you mustn't move.'

'Where's Paul?'

'Don't worry about Paul, just keep still. I don't think you've done anything very terrible to yourself but we don't want to take any chances. You've got a lovely bruise on your forehead. In a few hours it will be like brilliant Technicolor.'

'Don't treat me like a child,' she said tearfully. 'What are you playing at being today, Peter? A doctor. You're a good actor. What the critics would call a very convincing performance. What page of the secret service manual gives the instructions on how to make love to a traitor's wife? Will you get a decoration for this, Peter? An M.B.E. do you think? Surely not a knighthood. Oh, I hate you Peter Devlin.'

He put his arm underneath her shoulder and raised her head a little. 'Here,' he said, putting a flask to her lips, 'I'll risk the doctor's wrath and give you a sip of this. You need it.'

She gasped and spluttered as the brandy burned her throat. He held her against him and she had no will to pull away. She felt none of the expected revulsion; it was simply a comfort to be near him even now.

Over his shoulder she caught sight of a pall of smoke rising from below the line of the hill. 'Where is Paul?' she asked again and her voice was tremulous.

'I'm sorry, Francesca, but the car hit a tree and burst into flames. You were thrown out first, but he was still inside. The car was an inferno in seconds. I'm sorry,' he repeated, 'this time he really is dead.'

She closed her eyes, blotting out the

sight of that awful pall of smoke and, burying her head in the darkness of his shoulder, she cried.

★   ★   ★

Francesca threw the rest of her few belongings into the brand new suitcase. The nurse smiled and said in careful English, 'I hope, *madame*, the things I got for you were all right. It is difficult shopping for another.'

'They're fine,' answered Francesca. 'It was good of you to trouble on your half day.'

The nurse smiled again. Francesca knew she was being pitied for losing everything except the clothes she was wearing when the car caught fire. The nurse couldn't know that Francesca was delighted to have the last remnant of the past burned to ashes, ashes from which the phoenix would never rise.

The new clothes were far from elegant, reflecting the nurse's mundane taste, but they felt good against

Francesca's skin. She felt cleansed.

'The taxi will be here in a few minutes,' said the nurse. 'I'll let you know when it arrives.'

She closed the door quietly as she went. They had given Francesca a private room. It was very small, containing a bed and a metal locker, but it suited her needs. She just wanted to be alone.

She pushed her passport into her handbag and then closed the suitcase. As she did so the sunlight streaming in through the small window caught her wedding ring. Her hand froze over the lock for a moment and then she slipped the ring off, holding it in the palm of her hand for one brief second and then tossing it into the wastepaper basket. There was no feeling of regret, just relief.

The door opened and she turned to smile at the nurse. Her smile faded. She turned away again. 'Go away, Peter. I don't want to see you.'

He had discarded the casual clothes

of the holidaymaker. He looked businesslike and cold now, just as she remembered him at the airport. He stood squarely in front of her making no move to leave.

'That's the message I've been receiving for the past three days, and that's why I didn't bother to announce my arrival. This time I was in no mood for a further refusal.'

'We have nothing to say to each other. Besides, I have no time; a taxi is coming for me any moment now.'

'I've sent him away.'

She whirled round on him. 'You had no right to do that!'

'I'll take you wherever you want to go in my car. It's waiting outside.'

'I don't wish to go with you,' she said very deliberately and very slowly.

'Well, you have no choice now, have you? Where were you going anyway?'

'To the airport.'

'With no plane reservation?'

She gave a little gasp of impatience. 'I wasn't discharged until an hour ago.'

'How is the foot?'

'Still sore. The bump on my head turned out to be nothing, but two toes are broken where Paul crushed my foot down onto the brake pedal.'

He looked down at the floor. 'Yes, I know.'

Suddenly her apathy left her. 'You know everything about me, don't you? Even when I told you about my illness and everything that had happened to me, you already knew. You listened to me, pretended to sympathise, and all the time you *knew*.'

He gave a little sigh. 'I probably know more about you than you know yourself, Francesca, but I was interested in every word you uttered and it wasn't in the line of duty.'

He came to sit at the end of the bed but Francesca still stood stiffly at its side, not looking at him; never looking at him. 'You lied to me. You lied and lied all the time. Every minute we spent together was a lie.'

'I didn't lie about the important

things, Francesca.' When she didn't answer he asked resignedly, 'What do you want to do?'

'I'm going to wait at the airport for the first vacant seat on a flight to London.'

He reached into his inside pocket and, taking out a ticket, he threw it onto the bed at her side. She looked down at it but made no attempt to touch it.

'Before you say anything, I have its twin.'

'You're taking me back.' Her lips curled into a smile. 'Still under orders, Peter?'

'I'm going back to London. There would be no point in anyone else taking you, and equally no point in your travelling alone.'

'Am I under arrest?'

'Of course not. As far as anyone is concerned you were alone in that car. Your husband died six months ago.'

'I'm free?' she asked and her voice betrayed no particular interest.

'Of course.'

'What will happen to Chantal?'

'I'm afraid it has nothing to do with me. She admitted to tampering with the brakes. Paul showed her how to do it, but in the circumstances she can't be held responsible for his death. It's best for everyone to believe he died six months ago. I don't think they'll be hard on her. It will be treated as an accident. She's very lucky.'

Francesca gave a mirthless laugh. 'Poor Chantal. What will happen to the others?'

'Nothing. They knew nothing of his activities over the years until he came here.' Then he said briskly, 'What are you doing when you get back, Francesca?'

'I'll check in at a hotel for the time being. By now the agent should have found a prospective buyer for the lease of my flat; he can get rid of the furniture too. I want nothing. I don't even want his name. I'm changing it back to my maiden name, by deed poll.'

He traced the naked white line on

her finger where the wedding ring had been. As she snatched her hand away he said softly, 'I have a much better idea; you can change your name to mine as soon as you like.'

She gave a bitter little laugh. 'There's no need to go on, Peter. The act is over. I know this was just a job to you. You can take me back to London and then get on with the next job.'

'Yes, it was a job. I had orders to keep near you, find out if you were involved or not, and if Varonne was still alive and at the château.'

'And whose idea was it for you to pretend to fall in love with me?'

'No one's. It happened. I certainly never intended it to. Personal involvements are expressly forbidden; you should know that. The moment I spoke to you I hated this job, but even if I could have backed out it was too late. I *had* to go on with it despite my personal feelings. Try to understand, Francesca. If I'd told you the truth at any time, I'd have put you in an intolerable position.'

'Nothing could be more intolerable than what has happened.'

'Five days ago I told you I loved you. I loved you almost from the beginning, and my feelings haven't changed. What I want to know is, have yours?'

'Circumstances have changed.'

'Yes, you're finally free of him now. I wasn't sure of that then.'

'He said you'd kill him rather than let him get away. Is that true?'

His eyes looked into hers. 'Yes.'

'How many men have you killed?'

'None.'

'But you might do, one day. I'll always wonder about that, every time you come home.'

He smiled again. 'Oh no, Francesca. I'm all finished with that. I've allowed myself to become personally involved, and once is enough. I could have killed Paul Varonne simply for what he's done to you. That is why I'm finished with this job. That and having to live with the knowledge that you might have died with him, and it would have been my fault.'

'Your conscience needn't bother you, Peter,' she answered. 'I'm quite all right.'

'Are you?' he answered bitterly. 'I wish I'd never let you go back there.'

'To stop me you would have had to tell me you suspected Paul was alive, and if you had I'd have gone back anyway. I wouldn't have acted any differently, Peter. I wanted him to get away. By the time he'd finished telling me what he'd done, how he'd used us all, I hated him; but I was married to him for five years and there must have been something there to love even if it was only in my own mind. I wish with all my heart he'd got away.'

He said nothing for a moment. He took the plane ticket and put it into her handbag. Then he got to his feet. 'Do you want to see any of the Varonnes before you go back home?'

She shook her head. 'I don't think they'd want to see me.'

'Your mother-in-law blames you for all that happened, so perhaps you'd best not go.'

Francesca gave a little laugh. It was a harsh sound. 'If it gives her some comfort, I'm glad she does blame me.'

'Will you give me time, Francesca? Time to prove that I can be trusted. That's all I ask now.'

She turned away, pretending to check the labels on her suitcase. 'I had hoped you'd come with me to give the doll to Diana. I wrote to her the day we bought it and told her I'd be bringing someone home with me.'

'You had no right to do that.'

'Perhaps not, but you wouldn't want to disappoint a child, would you?'

'You're using unfair pressure.'

He put his arms around her and pressed his cheek to hers. 'I'd go to any lengths to see you happy again. Happy, and in love with me as you were the day we went to Ceyranne.'

For a moment she remained motionless in his arms, and then she twisted round. She let him hold her for a short time while before she pulled away, saying softly, 'If we're going to be in time for that plane we'd better go. It's time we were going home.'

THE END

We do hope that you have enjoyed reading this large print book.

Did you know that all of our titles are available for purchase?

We publish a wide range of high quality large print books including:
**Romances, Mysteries, Classics
General Fiction
Non Fiction and Westerns**

Special interest titles available in large print are:
**The Little Oxford Dictionary
Music Book, Song Book
Hymn Book, Service Book**

Also available from us courtesy of Oxford University Press:
**Young Readers' Dictionary
(large print edition)
Young Readers' Thesaurus
(large print edition)**

For further information or a free brochure, please contact us at:
**Ulverscroft Large Print Books Ltd.,
The Green, Bradgate Road, Anstey,
Leicester, LE7 7FU, England.
Tel:** (00 44) **0116 236 4325
Fax:** (00 44) **0116 234 0205**